The Horse Thief's Crime

By Wesley Ann

Chapter One

Sprinting hooves ate up the ground under Kaitlyn Heide's ink black mare. Dust leapt up behind them, clouding the one street of Dillon, Montana. The young woman's rebellious, dark gold hair worked its way out of her tight braid one strand at a time as her horse accelerated. She wasn't sure they had ever gone this fast before.

Just in front of them, a large stray steer was making his bid for freedom. The speckled, short-horn puffed heavily. He was nearing the outskirts of town and if Kaitlyn wasn't mistaken, the beast was on course to stampede straight over the yard of her one-room schoolhouse.

They were rapidly closing in. With her cobalt blue eyes locked on her target, Kaitlyn whipped the rope off her saddle horn and stood in her stirrups, leaning forward to watch for her chance.

"Come on, Dolly," she urged, "We've almost got him."

The bovine dodged left just in time to avoid crashing into the red brick school-house. Dolly's neck snaked out. She took one more giant stride to get into position. Kaitlyn let her lariat fly.

The loop sailed over one horn and then the other. Kaitlyn's fingers subconsciously dallied her end of the rope as she sat back firmly. Dolly simultaneously skidded to a halt, using all her weight to hold the steer back. The horse and rider both looked at their prize, beaming. The steer glared back at them, defeated.

He fought the rope all the way down main street as Kaitlyn and Dolly dragged him back to the Railroad's stockyard. A large herd of his kind was being funneled from one pen to another, preparing to be loaded onto the train. In all of the comotion, the cowboys working the beeves hadn't noticed her ride up.

"I believe this belongs to you," Kaitlyn called out. She addressed the man nearest the entry gate with an untidy black mustache and watery eyes. It was clear he was in charge of the outfit from his stature and his sparkling, silver-plated saddle.

"Not now, gal," he fussed, not bothering to turn around.

Kaitlyn's smile turned sour. "I'll just keep your cow, then," she yelled over the deafening bellering.

"What?" Confused, the surly cowboy finally took his attention off of counting his herd, which he hadn't been doing with much accuracy, to see that the woman just outside the gate had a rope around one of his steers.

"Where did you get that?" he muttered, looking down at the defeated short-horn. "Bring him through here." He opened the gate just wide enough for the cow to squeeze through but closed it before Kaitlyn and Dolly could follow, which left Kaitlyn no choice but to let go of her rope and watch as the speckled steer drug it through a deep patch of mud.

"I need my rope back," Kaitlyn protested.

Grudgingly, the ungrateful rancher rode up to pull the loop off of his steer's horns and re-coiled the now filthy rope. He walked his horse over to where Kaitlyn waited and passed it over the fence, finally taking a solid look at her for the first time.

He immediately averted his eyes at the sight of her split riding skirt.

"It's 1901," she mused at him. "If you're afraid of a split skirt, just wait until you see the new riding pants they're wearing in Helena."

He made a sort of scoffing sound. Then, he resumed counting his cattle, starting over from one.

Seeing that she wasn't going to get any sort of a thankyou, Kaitlyn wheeled her horse around. The town's vicious wind pinned the mare's forelock back, displaying a brilliant white star. The cowgirl raced Dolly down main street and past the schoolhouse, across the grass flats beyond, wondering if she could run faster yet.

That night, the wind outside of the schoolhouse was screaming murderously. Kaitlyn groaned. She peered outside at the grey hours of the night. Nondescript shadows crouched on the town's one street. The ground was sloppy with moisture that the dead soil wouldn't drink. One puddle after another. A pocket of wasteland in the middle of paradise. The dilapidated brick schoolhouse did little to provide comfort or shelter with its sagging roof and crowded quarters.

A leak in the roof nonchalantly welcomed thick raindrops about a foot away from the bed. The antique pitcher that caught them was painted with cheerful sunflowers and looked awkwardly out of place. The pitcher's spout faced the room's only window where more moisture found its way through the worn window sill and onto the corner of the bed quilt.

Many nights like this one, Kaitlyn awoke disoriented and confused. Pushing tangled hair out of her eyes, she began to recognize her current lot in life. She lay in a dark, run-down, excuse for a room. It's only furnishings aside from the bed were a small table with a broken leg and a mahogany chest from the old country, which contained her private collection of six books and two extra dresses.

Tonight, these facts came together quickly. On other nights, it took longer for the young schoolteacher to orient herself amidst the pounding wind and the tiny room. For entire nights, she would deceive herself into thinking that she was living in a nice room in a pretty town, teaching grammar to polite, angelic children.

Even in her short, cherished glimpses of sleep, Kaitlyn's thoughts echoed the words of her grandfather, an old German immigrant, who had been heartbroken to see her leave home. He had asked her time and time again to reconsider. Somehow, he had known right from the start that staying on their family ranch would have been a better life for a girl than taking a chance on Dillon. If only she'd listened to him.

A dry farm town's version of paying well was not the same as Kaitlyn's. The children were miserably ill-behaved when they did come to school. The young teacher wasn't sure why she hadn't left earlier. At this point, she was too poor to buy provisions for the trip home. As the windstorm outside howled on, Kaitlyn drifted back into a shallow sleep.

When dawn finally came to Dillon, it was not a relief, but at least the wind had let up. Each day in Dillon was a trade between waiting for the morning when the wind would stop howling and then waiting for the afternoon when the school children would disappear out into the renewed wind, nearly blowing away in their escape home.

It wasn't uncommon for the older kids to trickle out before the day's lessons were over. This mutiny frustrated Kaitlyn to no end, but she had learned that there was no use in trying to keep them if they had no desire to stay. Once the older kids, especially the boys, had lost interest in mathematics and grammar, they worked steadily on their project of destroying the schoolhouse.

The sons of the railroad station owner, Judd and Jeremiah Wylie, would pull out pocket knives and carve away at the wooden desks when Kaitlyn's back was turned. It all seemed very systematic. By her estimation, if any of the kids made it to eighth grade, they would have no more desks to write at, and at that point, they would have the perfect excuse to go home.

Determined to seize just a few minutes of peace before becoming the wrangler of twelve unruly children, Kaitlyn pulled on a steel blue dress and hurried outside. The land was quiet. Sparse blades of grass bent sideways in the schoolyard, exhausted from the wind's constant battering. The blades skipped farther down the street, joining up with a row of identically crooked trees.

For no particularly good reason, it was hard to look at the town in the morning. It was beautiful in its own way. The storefronts proudly presented shining silver bridles, new cotton ropes, and ornate saddles only a cattle baron could afford. Perhaps it was knowing the precious stillness was just a temporary façade that gave even the mornings A bitter taste.

At the end of town, the stockyards lead up to the railroad. Cattle drives of all sizes came to Dillon to load their livestock on the train. Jonathan Beauford Wyle, the railroad yard owner, often met the cattle drives horseback to explain he could only offer a portion of the advertised price for their cattle. Wylie dressed like a cowboy and presented himself as a businessman, but the way he sat in the saddle and the business deals he made were both ten different kinds of crooked.

Kaitlyn felt in her pocket for the well-worn letter from Jonathan Wylie that had lured her here. She unfolded the thick yellow parchment.

Dearest Miss Heide,

I am writing to you in regards to a school teaching position in the town of Dillon. Joshua Challis spoke highly of your education. Our school teacher passed away last winter, leaving our children without guidance. My two young sons are among them. The schoolhouse is newly rebuilt with large living quarters. Compensation is generous. I eagerly await your reply.

Please give my best regards to your grandfather
Jonathan Beauford Wylie

That was that. Kaitlyn had accepted, thinking only of Mr. Wylie's two sons and the other poor children without a teacher. There were still kids in parts of Montana who could barely read. Who would teach them if she didn't? Kaitlyn had always felt like there was a greater purpose for her out there somewhere. Perhaps this was it.

It soon became apparent that Mr. Wylie, who was himself recently widowed, had other things on his mind. Somehow, in his general education, he had missed the fact that it was inappropriate for a school teacher to marry. With his hopes of finding a second wife dashed, the cheapskate decided to slash Kaitlyn's already modest wages.

Kaitlyn shook her head, returning to the real world. She rounded the corner of the schoolhouse, gingerly avoiding muddy puddles. Built off the backside of the living quarters was a wooden corral and a pathetic overhang that kept some of the rain off of a six-foot-wide area, providing the moisture didn't blow down sideways. A tall, ink-black horse stood on the tiny dry patch of ground beneath — her four white socks were miraculously clean.

"Breakfast time, Dolly," Kaitlyn called to her.

The black mare stepped forward in response, poking her head out into the soft sunlight. A sizable drop of water raced down the overhang, splashing onto the white star on her forehead. Dolly pinned her ears back flat against her head. She shook the water out of her dark forelock sharply, looking rather offended.

"You needed a bath anyway," Kaitlyn teased as she tossed a thick flake of hay over the fence. Dolly began to nuzzle through the feed, searching for alfalfa leaves hidden among the stems. Her soft eyes and gentle expression drew Kaitlyn's attention, dissolving the rest of the world. There was something so relaxing and mesmerizing about Dolly. She was like the eye of a storm embodied on four legs. Life could be tumultuous, but in the middle of the storms, there was always that calm eye where it was once again possible to breathe.

The peace didn't last. A chorus of boisterous shouts rose from down the town's main street. Kaitlyn looked over her shoulder to see three large cow-ponies prancing down the dirt towards the schoolhouse. Even from a distance, the morning sunlight flooded into the ornately tooled leather breast collars on the three ponies.

Two boys in black felt hats aggressively rode the matching sorrels leading the way. A red roan followed reluctantly behind, its ears pinned periodically as a tiny blonde girl urged it forward. As the trio made their way towards the schoolhouse, the features of the three Wylie kids became clearer.

The Wylie kids rode to school though they lived within walking distance. While most town folks sent their kids to school on foot, that wouldn't do for Mr. Wylie's kids. The sons of the stockyard owner, Jeremiah, and Judd, both wore oversized silver spurs that were mostly useless on their poorly behaved mounts. If anything, the spurs were good for scratching up schoolhouse chairs and poking their sister. The little blonde girl trailed sheepishly behind them wherever they went, not exactly willing to go but less willing to be left behind alone.

Kaitlyn composed herself. She walked to the hitching rail, grabbing three get-down ropes from a nearby bucket. Judd and Jeremiah clumsily bullied their sorrel ponies up to the fence and dismounted, throwing their reins over and under in what couldn't quite be considered an actual knot. In the same attempt she made every day, Kaitlyn spoke up.

"Jedidiah, Jeremiah, do you think you should fetch some water for your horses?"

"School teachers got to take care of them," Jeremiah announced, gesturing to his horse.

"Have to," Kaitlyn corrected. Neither of them seemed to notice she had spoken.

"Montana law," Judd chimed in.

Before their teacher could get another word in, the boys raced off into the schoolyard. Kaitlyn was left wondering if such boys in fifth and sixth grade should be in school after all. Some real work could have done them good. Of course, they would never know any real work, and certainly not any discipline, as the sons of Mr. Wylie.

Returning her attention to the road, Kaitlyn found that Darla's red roan had stopped two hundred feet short of the hitching rail at a patch of tall grass. Her six-year-old legs barely long enough to span the mare's broad back, Darla didn't have much of a way to make the uncooperative horse go forward. Kaitlyn went to the child's rescue. She looped one of the get down ropes just behind the mare's head, around her throat latch, and marched the disgruntled roan the rest of the way to the school.

In one swift motion, the former ranch girl tied the get-down rope in a slip knot around the hitching rail. Darla stretched her arms down for her teacher who delivered her from the saddle to the ground.

"Miss Kaitlyn, do you want me to get water for Minnie?" Darla asked. Her innocent blue eyes didn't have a mean speck in them.

"No, that's alright, Darla. You run along and play until school starts," Kaitlyn answered. With her blonde curls bobbing, Darla raced after her brothers. She wouldn't have been able to lift a full water bucket if she'd tried.

Taking an assessment of Minnie, Kaitlyn noticed that the ornery mare's red coloring reflected her temperament. Why anyone would choose such a horse for a child was beyond Kaitlyn's understanding. Mr. Wylie bought the most expensive colts he could find. The problem was that he and his boys weren't much for horse handlers or gentlemen and the animals all started to act just as rude as their owner after a few weeks. The sorrels might have been respectable citizens if not for their handling, but Minnie was plain mean.

Kaitlyn began detangling the mess of reins that Judd and Jeremiah had left on the hitching rail. The school teacher generally disliked tying horses by their reins. Though the Wylie kids neglected to bring any safe tying mechanism, lest they should endanger their rough cowboy persona, Kaitlyn had eventually made the get-down ropes mandatory. Their sorrel ponies had collectively broken three sets of reins that year, pulling them loose from the rail and stomping on them or pulling hard enough on their reins to bend the bit.

It was technically, by law, the school teacher's responsibility to care for any horses that the children rode to school. The task of furnishing water buckets, removing bridles, and loosening cinches had become Kaitlyn's barrier between the children's arrival and the real beginning of the school day. A few other students trickled in, mostly on foot. Two dark skinned girls from a nearby ranch rode in quietly, hitched their horses, and walked into the school without a word. Other kids congregated in twos and threes in the schoolyard.

Soon, all twelve of the regular students were present. Kaitlyn wrapped her fist around the unraveling strand of twine tied to the school's repurposed dinner bell. The rusty old bell clamored reluctantly.

The Wylie brothers slowly looked up from their marble game but didn't move. Little Darla glanced sheepishly between her older siblings. "School's started," she whispered to them. Judd glared at her and lined up another shot. Versicolored marbles scattered. Kaitlyn rang the bell again.

Seeing that he was about to lose the game anyway, Jeremiah scooped up a handful of marbles and strode to the school. Judd tucked the rest of the marbles in his pocket triumphantly. Darla tugged at his shirt sleeve. Once their pack leaders had gone inside, the remaining children followed suit.

Thirteen dusty wooden chairs resided in the school. It was a full day. The twelve kids managed to fill all of them. Judd used the thirteenth as a footrest, occasionally pushing Jeremiah's boots off of the edge when he tried to invade.

Summoning her patience, Kaitlyn began to write on the cracked chalkboard.

Rejoice in the Lord O ye righteous

"What's ye?" Sam Pickett, who sat in the front row, asked.

"It's like yee haw" a girl named Loraine whispered behind him.

Sam seemed satisfied with the explanation and returned to his scribbling. Sam was one of the older boys left in school due to a badly mangled left hand that had been caught in some piece of farm equipment or other over the summer. The lack of two good hands made him poor help at home. Mrs. Pickett must have had a horrible time trying to keep up on work without him.

Upon Sam's return to school, he began scribbling with his good hand and hadn't ceased ever since. It was becoming a real problem. He was going through more paper than the school had to spare.

Kaitlyn couldn't help but smile at the ridiculous explanation.

"That's an excellent guess, Loraine," she offered. "It's not right though. In the King James Bible, the word ye is used instead of the word you."

Kaitlyn eagerly wrote another psalm, hoping she had found something to engage the class's attention.

Things did not exactly go as planned. For the rest of the day, the children referred to each other as "ye," and, "thou." Jeremiah could be heard in the schoolyard yelling, "Ye take that!" as he and Judd destroyed burgeoning ant hills.

When Kaitlyn attempted to call the students in from their recess, Judd puffed up his chest, announcing, "Pa needs us to cowboy for him this afternoon."

"Oh, that's nice," Kaitlyn tried to humor him, unsure if the excuse was true. "Well, you go along then, and the rest of the kids can come inside."

Judd had a mischievous look in his eye like a calf who had found a way to escape from his pen. "Pa said he needs as many as he can get," he announced loudly. He bounded out of sight, dragging Jeremiah along by the shirtsleeve. Darla skittered to catch up.

Though she had a soft spot for Darla, it didn't particularly bother Kaitlyn to see those two boys off. Now perhaps there would be some focus in the classroom. The teacher stepped back inside for just a moment to find her mathematics book. She would ring the bell and mean it this time. Everyone would listen to her. She marched outside with determination.

The yard was deserted. At the very edge of the town, a handful of short figures kicked up clouds of grey dust. The afternoon sun glinted off of Judd and Jeremiah's silver hat bands as they led the way.

Kaitlyn sank into a desk chair, shoulders hunched. Why didn't any of her students listen? Though Kaitlyn secretly feared she was a lousy teacher, lack of manners certainty played a role. The town of Dillon also had a strange air about it that seeped in with the school kids. It sometimes seemed like the impending truth that life would be bleak and plain, with or without an eighth-grade diploma, had already occurred to all of them. After all, a dusty farm in a windy county led to only more days in the wind until the ultimate return to the dust.

Trying each new day had become a monumental feat. Kaitlyn's morale was exhausted, and if she had been any less stubborn, she would have just given in and married Mr. Wylie to get out of the leaking schoolhouse.

"I shouldn't be here," she explained to the floor. "It's no wonder I'm miserable when I shouldn't be here." As she looked around, her eyes came to rest on the chalkboard.

It still read *Rejoice in the Lord*

"I suppose I ought to take my advice," she said to herself. Kaitlyn rose slowly, her body mechanically entering her room and shedding the steel blue dress for a split riding skirt while her mind wandered. She emerged with her blonde bun freshly tightened; a bridle balanced over her shoulder; her arms tucked around a heavy saddle.

As evening came, the wind welcomed itself into the gaps between Kaitlyn's scarf and coat. She galloped Dolly recklessly across the barren hills. The black mare dodged stumpy prickly pear cactus gracefully, increasing her speed with each stride. Kaitlyn leaned low over the saddle horn, thrilled and horrified by the breakneck pace.

In her mind, she imagined traversing the hundreds of miles back to the home ranch, racing until the unwelcoming landscape was far behind. Her imagination finally turned Dolly loose in the lush mountain pasture far to the north, but her body stopped short and reluctantly turned back to another lonely night at the school.

Chapter Two

Hundreds of miles north, black tree outlines blended with the predawn sky. Josh pulled on one lived-in cowboy boot after the other and extended his lanky legs to stretch out the morning stiffness. A short survey of the bunkhouse turned up his crooked brown felt hat. It needed reshaping as badly as the bunkhouse did, but both of those things were at the bottom of a long list that never got done.

Taking the last swig of his morning coffee, Josh compiled a mental list of morning chores. He would make his rounds in the top pastures before breakfast to see if any heifers needed help having their calves. Thanks to a neighbor's poor fences and determined Black Angus bull, a large number of the calves born so far had been black with white faces. The Baldies frustrated the Boss, who ran only Hereford cattle, to no end. Josh chuckled. He personally found the little Baldie calves amusing, but he kept that to himself.

Josh closed the creaky bunkhouse door behind him. He paused for a moment to pull his fleece collar tight against the frigid cold. Snow still clung to the shadowy barnyard, adjacent to the bunkhouse. Come summertime, the shade would be a welcome haven from the dry Montana sun, but for now, it only slowed the process of wishing another winter farewell.

Out in the low pastures just past the yard, the snow was nearly gone. Red and white mother cows dotted the landscape, nursing their small calves. Pregnant heifers sat amidst them, lazily chewing their cud. Across the valley, mountains jutted upward, the high peaks like wolf teeth taking a bite out of the clouds.

It was unusual for Josh to be the last one out of the bunkhouse. Being second out was a shame. It meant Garrett had a head start and Garret was hard enough to keep track of when they started at the same time. Josh had at least a few jobs to do that would have been much easier with a second man and no clue where the ranch's other residents were.

Josh didn't make a habit of complaining if he could help it, but it would have been nice to have some idea of what was going on. The Boss and Garrett always wandered off without consulting anyone, and yet each always seemed to know where the other would be. Josh, on the other hand, didn't share their connection. He had to go looking.

When he had saddled Old Bay and started into the first winter pasture, Josh spotted a figure halfway down the fence line. A stocky-shouldered man knelt in the remaining snow next to the barbwire. As Josh trotted his big bay gelding closer, the figure looked up in acknowledgment and then returned his attention to the fence.

"Good morning," Josh offered, testing the ranch owner's mood.

The man in the snow wore a stern look on his face. Hard wrinkles creased his square jawline. Peppered black hair was just visible beneath his heavy Scotch cap. If he couldn't nail the barbwire back to its post, he could probably give it a harsh enough glare to scare it back into line.

Another figure, equally stocky but much taller, stood suddenly, causing Josh's bay to spook backward a few steps. Josh tensed, instantly drawing his hand down one rein to tip his horse's nose around. Both rider and horse let out a sigh, taking in the realization that it was only the other hired hand, Garret.

"I see you're too cowboy to get off and help fix a fence," Garret teased.

"You don't have to get me off my horse that way," Josh said, dismounting. "You know Old Bay hates surprises. What do you have to scare him for?"

"You should thank me. I'm helping desensitize him. I thought you horsemen who are too high and mighty to fix fences with the rest of us loved that kind of stuff."

"I thought I was too cowboy. Now I'm a horseman?"

"No, no. I misspoke," Garret corrected himself. "If you were a horseman your horse there wouldn't be afraid of nothing. You're more of a buckaroo."

"I've never been to the Great Basin," Josh protested.

"So what's that got to do with it? Buy a flat-brimmed hat, and you're part of the group. That poor hat you got on now would do the trick if you let a couple more cows step on it."

Josh simply scowled.

"A wrangler?" Garret suggested. "Cowpuncher? Oh! I know. You're a cattleman. Cattleman is at least a step up from cowboy."

"Don't the cattlemen own the cattle?" Josh pointed out.

"That doesn't leave me with a whole lot to call you," Garret complained. His eyes danced with mischief. Giving Josh a bad time was one of the very few forms of entertainment Garrett got on the ranch.

"Whatever you two are or aren't called you're wasting daylight," the Boss finally cut in.

Garret dug a couple of nails out of his pocket. Balancing one between his teeth, he began to pound the other into the nearest post. "Aw, don't worry about that," Garret mumbled around the fencing nail. "I'm a multi-tasker. The only ranch hand in two counties who can work hard and talk good at the same time."

"I wish I had been warned of that before I hired you," the Boss said. He still seemed bent on his task, but he was failing to conceal a faint smile.

Garret could somehow get away with smart talking the Boss, a feat that would have gotten any other man fired. Many suspected it was because Garret's tall, broad figure and dark

Germanic eyes reminded the Boss of his only son, whom he occasionally visited in the cemetery.

Garret had arrived in the county as a shaggy sixteen-year-old not long after William Heide had been laid to rest beside his wife, Charlotte and baby boy, Samuel. Something in young Garret's appearance and demeanor said that he would someday grow to fill the role William Heide's passing had left open. He would never be a Heide, but he didn't need to be. The livestock and the family accepted him.

The Boss did have two other children, daughters, who had both jumped at their first chance to marry businessmen. Neither had set a high-heeled shoe on the ranch in over twenty years. It was the only son, Kaitlyn's late father, who had been the Boss's one hope of keeping the ranch in the family. Now even Kaitlyn Heide, the last of her namesake, seemed to have left the ranching life behind.

It was the mention of his granddaughter that finally drew John Heide to his feet.

"Have you heard from Kaitlyn?" Garret asked Josh.

The Boss interjected before Josh could answer. "You went to town yesterday?"

"Yes, sir."

"Was there a letter?"

Josh only shook his head, watching light snowflakes begin to settle on his boots. He could see the disappointment spread over the Boss's countenance. It had been many weeks since the last letter, which happened to be dated nearly a month before its actual arrival.

"I'm sure she'll write to us soon," Josh offered.

"Well I'm sure she already did," the Boss said. He turned from his task and leaned against a fence post. "It's the Dillon Post Office. They probably tried to send it to Helena, Alabama instead of Helena, Montana. Again."

As if to frustrate him further, the fence post sagged sideways, the ground that had once held it upright shifting as the earth thawed. The Boss stumbled a step backward before regaining his balance. An irritated look flooded his face. He seemed ready to launch into a long tirade but then changed his mind, and stopped short of it. "I hope neither of you have been asking God to teach you about patience," he said. "Mine is being tested today."

Josh and Garret looked back and forth between themselves. The Boss was in no way a patient man, only stubborn and persistent. Of course, both hired men had the good sense not to mention that. Instead, they returned to their tasks. Josh swung back onto his horse, squeezing his legs around the bays' belly, and trotted off.

The low pastures were an ever-changing color palette. Patches of snow shown almost blue, reflecting the early morning light. A long strip of pale yellow straw had been spread right down the middle of the land for the cattle to use as bedding. Massive mountains to the east that curved around the ranch nearly blocked the sunrise. Only the boldest of oranges and pinks found their way through the low saddles on the ridge. Nearby, pure white icicles hung off the barbwire fence.

The fence line was oddly shaped to encompass the winding mountain stream that trickled along even in the dead of winter. The water flowed from a hot spring at the edge of the mountains where it boiled out of the ground. Between the initial temperature and all the two-foot waterfalls along its path, the water never froze.

Josh, however, did freeze. By the time he had established that none of the new heifers planned on having their calves anytime that morning, he sorely wished he had piled on more layers of clothing. His solid felt vest and black silk wild rag still hung back in the bunkhouse where they weren't doing anybody any good. Josh finished up his round quickly. He pulled his saddle off of Old Bay and leaned up against the horse closely, absorbing the gelding's body heat. The sunrise crested the great mountains.

That night, the smell of burnt game meat wafted into the dining room. Garret had turned his back to the cook stove for just a moment to glance through the small museum of catalogs and flyers collecting in the main house. One advertised a Wild West show being put on nearby. The brochure promised excitement with a bucking horse contest, sharpshooting, and world-class steer roping. With interest, Garret turned the flyer over to check the date. The event had already happened nearly six months ago. With a huff, he tossed the flyer on the dusty wooden floor.

"Why is half the mail in here a year old?" Garrett hollered over his shoulder.

"I'll tell you if you tell me why supper's burning," the Boss called back from the next room.

Garret rolled his eyes, dismissing the regular complaints about his cooking. Since Mrs. Heide had fallen sick in the fall, someone had to take up the task of providing breakfast, dinner, and supper. Garret was perhaps the least qualified of the men on the ranch as he continually underestimated the attention cooking required. He was, however, the most enthusiastic about trading in outside chores in subzero temperatures to cozy up to the cook stove. In exchange, Josh and the Boss regularly sat down to undercooked, burnt, or completely ashen food.

Josh poked his head into the kitchen just in time to see smoke start rising from the elk meat. It wafted up the home's chinked log walls into beautifully hemmed window curtains. Josh sighed in frustration and moved the skillet off to the side. He took three steaks off- two for himself and one for the Boss- and strode back to the living room table.

Garret stayed in the kitchen to tend the stew he had prepared for Mrs. Heide. Chicken stock boiled around chunks of potatoes and wild roots. Josh and the Boss could be heard talking over their tooth-breaking meal.

"Ranchers have always been too poor to afford their own steaks," the Boss said. He bit off a sizeable chunk of his well-done elk meat and chewed laboriously before continuing. "With the way the elk help themselves to my haystack all winter, I almost feed more to them than to the cows."

There was some truth to the statement. No amount of fencing had yet succeeded in keeping a local elk herd out of the Heide Ranch's haystacks. The elk came and went as they pleased, oblivious to any unwelcome feelings from ranchers. Unlike the deer, elk didn't bother to jump over fences. Instead, the beasts waded through wooden rails like they didn't even exist. The damage could be catastrophic, but the easy game meat almost made up for the nuisance- when it wasn't burnt.

"Well, they almost feed us more than the cows," Garret called, adding another pinch of salt to the soup pot that still boiled atop the stove.

"Nope. I haven't ever had milk or cream from an elk," Josh argued. John Heide smiled.

When the Boss had finished his supper, he took Garret's place looking over the stove. Garrett sat down to his steak as Josh scraped every last scrap of meat and grease out of the skillet. While the boys ensured nothing went to waste, John Heide scooped up more soup than his wife could possibly eat and made his way to the back of the house.

Dorothy Heide lay in bed under a thick patchwork quilt. Her figure was small and frail, even beneath the mass of fabric. Uncombed black hair hung loosely around her shoulders.

Her cobalt blue eyes held the slightest hint of joy despite her pale cheeks. At John's approach, she sat up against a nest of pillows. The sight of John comforted her heart.

John Heide gently placed the bowl in Dorothy's hands. She wasn't sick with anything that a doctor could diagnose. The physicians who had seen her couldn't explain why she continued to survive with hardly a drop of energy, and yet there she was. John Heide had even paid for the best doctor in the state to come all the way from Helena. He was no help. Nobody who should have had knowledge on the subject seemed to know anything.

Only Dorothy, who was legendary for her ability to nurture a sick calf or mend any equine injury, appeared to have an innate understanding of her condition. She believed her body was fighting itself. She also had firm faith that the Lord would renew her strength in the proper time.

In the meantime, she passed her days quietly in the house. Dorothy had a content nature. On days when she felt more energetic, she would clean this or that. She wrote letters to family and former ranch help that she and John hadn't seen face to face in many years.

Dorothy's mother hen tendencies led her to take in folks who needed a real friend. John Heide often found gritty ranchers and their wives stopping to have iced tea and visit dear Mrs. Heide when they wandered through the territory.

There were also days when Dorothy could scarcely get out of bed. She twisted in pain, trying to crunch down the ailment hiding somewhere in her organs. Lying precariously close to the fire or pressing ice wrapped in a towel against her torso were the only tricks that relieved some of the symptoms.

When the worst of it had subsided, she usually sat in a wicker chair by the bedroom window, watching the cattle and horses outside in the snow. She waited for night time when John would lay close beside her and hold her hand as they both fell asleep.

They had been married since the age of eighteen and though even their marriage had been through its rough times, the fifty-four years they had been granted so far didn't seem like much time together to them. Dorothy still surprised John. Every time he was sure that he knew her, he would look a little harder and find out that there was more.

The rancher's wife had once discovered an old fiddle at a junk store in Helena. It was just her luck that the wife of the cowboy who had been their foreman at the time knew how to play it. When the men were outside putting up hay, the women would sneak out their instruments to practice. John never realized what the women folk had been doing inside until he came into the house early one day to hear a symphony pouring from the kitchen.

"I don't think you're the same woman I married," he had told Dorothy, teasingly giving her a pinch as if to make sure she was real.

"Well, I should certainly hope not" she'd replied. "What a silly thing to fuss over. If we're not changing, we're not growing, and that's not good for anyone."

Today's only change seemed to be that Dorothy weighed a little bit less than the day before. She drank up her soup dutifully, but John could see that even that was laborious for her. Neither of them could seem to find something to say. John stopped himself several times from asking, "How are you feeling?" because he didn't want to hear the answer. He wanted the answer to be that Dorothy was revived and felt just as strong as a summer sunflower. He longed to see her out of bed with her hair brushed back in a beautiful braid, her cobalt colored eyes hungry for the adventure life had in store. Most of all, he didn't want to hear the truth- that she was fading.

Eventually, Dorothy asked, "Did you have any new calves today?"

"Just two," John answered.

"Two calves," Dorothy repeated.

The room fell back into silence.

Finally, John ran his weathered hand over her black hair and said, "I'll be to bed soon."

Josh and Garrett were standing in the kitchen when John Heide came to return the soup bowl. Garret was drying off plates his careless handling had steadily chipped over the last winter while Josh boiled water for coffee. It was Josh's custom to make a fresh thermos of coffee before he took the first shift of night calving. He made it with over twice the recommended amount of coffee grounds and topped it off with heavy cream to make matters worse. Garret insisted that even just one cup of Josh's coffee could burn a hole in a buffalo's stomach. No one had ever been able to test the buffalo theory, but Josh had plenty of use for the coffee just the same.

The Boss stopped short, staring out the window.

"Boys, I think we've got trouble," he said. He didn't have to say much more. "Trouble," could only mean one thing during the calving season.

Grabbing a kerosene lamp from the porch, Garrett darted into the yard. A cold snap had rolled in that night. The temperature felt like five degrees above zero, warm by Montana winter standards but cold for late March. Still, the unpredictable weather was typical. The snow usually melted slowly with the weeks. Spring tended to coyly retreat back into scattered winter storms until March had nearly passed. The landscape always froze and melted again and again.

Garrett's dark green eyes quickly focused in on trouble at the near end of the low pasture. A dumb cow had dumped her calf directly into a snowbank. Its first few minutes in the world had been spent rapidly freezing to death. Josh hurried to catch Old Bay while Garret rushed into the field to find out if the calf was still alive.

The ranch hand reached the snow bank in record time. There wasn't much motion in the little red and white calf to indicate whether he was alive or dead — his eyes were rolled back in his head. His wet fur was frozen rigid. Garret couldn't help wondering if the calf had been stillborn. Placing a hand on the calf's chest, he felt the slightest rise and fall of breath. It was alive after all.

"We need to get some air in you, little bull," Garrett told the calf. He kept a wary eye on the mother cow while he began vigorously rubbing the calf to warm him up.

In minutes, Josh appeared, riding Old Bay, dragging a wooden sled with added side rails tacked on.

"Is she protective?" Josh yelled, gesturing to the mother cow. So far, the oblivious Hereford hadn't taken any interest in her calf.

"We'll be alright," Garret replied. He hoisted the calf onto the sled and stepped back just in time. The mother cow had suddenly decided to claim ownership of her calf. She pawed at the snow, sniffing the sled suspiciously. Josh gave Old Bay the cue to get going, and they trotted out of the way.

The angry mother cow charged along behind, bumping into Old Bay's hind legs when she caught up. Luckily, Old Bay was big enough and patient enough not to mind.

"At least she has some maternal instinct," Josh thought. They reached the barn where Josh laid the newborn Hereford calf in a thick bed of straw. Garret expertly slammed the stall door then closed the main barn entry, trapping the ornery cow in the alleyway. They would need her contained in a moment.

Josh took down a thick roll of wool from a manger turned storage shelf in the corner of the stall and began using it to dry the calf off. He manually pumped the calf's legs, hoping to spark some circulation. The calf's chest still rose and fell faintly, but his breath wasn't getting stronger; it was getting weaker.

"Give me a hand in here," he yelled to Garrett.

Garret slipped inside the stall, narrowly missing an attack from the mother cow who was pacing in the barn alley. The ranch hand took one look at the calf, dry and warm and still inches from death, and knew what needed to be done.

The two men each grabbed one of the calf's hind legs, lifting him up-side-down. They shook the creature firmly with his back hooves high in the air and his nose inches off of the ground. Sure enough, a thin drizzle of liquid escaped through the calf's mouth as he dangled. When he was returned to earth, his chest rose and fell with a stronger, steadier rhythm.

A clean set of lungs turned out to be what the calf had needed all along. He began to blink his eyes, slowly taking in everything around him. Josh kept his hands moving about the calf's back, but at this point, it was mostly to warm his own frozen fingertips.

"I think he'll make it if he gets some colostrum," Josh said. The thick, vital colostrum milk that cows produced for only a short time after calving could make all the difference in the world for a weak calf.

Working in a tired daze, the men tried introducing the mother and calf. Neither bovine had a clue what to do with the other. It eventually became apparent that someone would have to intervene for the calf to get anything into his stomach. Even after the mother cow had been trapped in a chute where she had to hold still, the calf couldn't be convinced to drink.

Garrett exhibited his wild-cow-milking skills and quickly had enough colostrum to fill a bottle that he force-fed the calf. At first, the calf squirmed and struggled against being bottle fed, but once the warm milk hit his stomach, his attitude changed. The pair still didn't understand each other, but at least the calf would survive the night.

"I think my shift's up" Josh mentioned. "I can stay out and keep an eye on this pair though."

Garret shook his head. "No, you get some sleep. I'll recheck these two after I do my round. There were a couple more cows that looked like they might calve tonight and I want to make sure they use the straw we put outside for them."

True to his word, Garret returned to the barn after he had made an uneventful tour of the pasture. He came in just in time to catch the calf happily nursing. The newborn bovine wore a white milk mustache as he settled back into the straw to rest. Garret headed for the bunkhouse to get a few hours of rest for himself.

Chapter Three

Bubbles clung to the skin between Kaitlyn's fingers. She sat inside the schoolhouse with a large washtub before her. She had moved a couple of desks to the side of the room to make a space for the cumbersome object. It was old enough that it should have been put out of its misery by its first owner. The boards would have made good fire kindling, but instead, it had been passed down to the school teacher one week when the town couldn't pay her salary. It leaked immediately.

The washboard was too old and feeble to work. If Kaitlyn scrubbed hard enough to break the dirt loose, the boards would groan and threaten to crack. Soon, Kaitlyn wished that she had just gone to the Chinese woman in town who took in washing and paid the money to have it done. The day seemed very utterly wasted.

Before the clothes could quite be considered clean, Kaitlyn gave up on the impossible project. She marched her washing around to the back of the schoolhouse where a low-hanging clothesline was spread between two fencing posts. She double-pinned each garment to the line, crossing her fingers that the strong afternoon wind wouldn't carry them away. The one upside to the wind was that it dried clothes very quickly if it didn't rip them off the line. With the last stocking hung, Kaitlyn hoped to salvage some of her day.

Kaitlyn had taken to knitting on Lacey Asbury's porch on Saturday afternoons. She didn't particularly like Lacey, but she preferred the company to being alone. The young woman was silly and didn't seem to have much in her head, but she offered lemonade and was an excellent knitter. Her porch even faced away from the wind.

From the moment the women were seated with their knitting baskets, Lacey droned on and on about gossip, and Kaitlyn didn't care to keep track of details. It wasn't entirely bad that Lacey considered Kaitlyn such a good listening ear. It kept Kaitlyn from having to come up with much to contribute to the trifling conversation. An occasional agreeing comment was all Lacey needed to carry on chatting all by herself. Kaitlyn primarily sipped her lemonade and took deep breaths of the relatively relaxing time.

"Word on the street is that farm boy Thomas Ferguson is going to try to marry the oldest Sterling daughter," Lacey whispered loudly, leaning in towards Kaitlyn. "Can you imagine a pretty girl like her marrying that poor sharecropper? Oh, it's just ridiculous."

"Well, maybe she likes him," Kaitlyn said plainly.

"I'm sure her father won't allow it," Lacey continued. "Thomas is not the sort of respectable man I would let my daughter marry, what with that little shack of a house he has. He's been out here on his own for two years, and all he has to show for it is a hay field and that dinky cabin. It's just not the sort of thing a proper wife can live in."

Kaitlyn bit her tongue and glanced behind herself at Lacey's house. There was a trick to satisfying Lacey. When she was told that something was expensive, she would love and treasure it. The ditzy town girl never could figure out whether a dress was costly or cheap without seeing the price tag.

This trick was how her husband, who was only a modestly wealthy man, kept her content. The Asbury home wasn't much more to speak of than Thomas Ferguson's, save some decorating, but Lacey didn't know that. Lacey fancied herself a wealthy woman, and it wasn't worth it to burst her misperception.

"I don't know if I see what his house has to do with it," Kaitlyn finally said. "It looks cozy enough to me, and farming's as good of a way to spend your life as any. How could Mr. Sterling turn Thomas down?"

Lacey was quite convinced that there were many reasons, including comfort, money, and most importantly, status. She began to tell Kaitlyn all about it, but Kaitlyn tuned her out to focus on her knitting project.

Down the street, Kaitlyn glimpsed the tall figure of Mr. Wylie disappearing into a saddle maker's store. The store owner, Bob Campbell, had been a Wild West show performer in his day. He displayed a photo of himself riding Roman with one leg each on two giant Percheron geldings above his counter. A riding accident had rendered his leg useless not far into his career, and he had taken up saddle making as a way to stay connected to the cowboy world.

Bob made saddles as lofty as the tricks he had once performed. The unsurpassed tooling had no practical purpose, save adding a pretty extra penny to the price tag, but it amazed and impressed any onlookers. Friendship with a nearby silversmith added even more elaborate decoration to the tack Bob had for sale or trade. Bob loved to trade.

Jonathan Wylie emerged carrying a thick paper sack. Kaitlyn could only imagine the money he'd casually thrown at whatever was inside. His bold black mustache was trimmed perfectly – a testament to his regular barber visit.

"Oh look, Kate," Lacey squealed. Her tightly curled auburn hair bounced as she rocked forward in her chair. "It's your beau!"

"Lacey, please don't call me that. You know I hate being called Kate." Of course, reminding Lacey was fruitless. Lacey didn't remember any thoughts that didn't come from her head, and there weren't very many of those. Lacey was insistent that Kaitlyn needed a rich husband just as badly as she needed a trendy Sunday dress. The importance of the character inside the man didn't seem to occur to Lacey, only the pocketbook.

"I'm also not looking for a suitor, especially not that one," Kaitlyn added. She had spoken up too late. Lacey was already enthusiastically waving Mr. Wylie over. He smiled widely at the invitation, showing a set of perfectly white but crooked front teeth.

Mr. Wylie caught sight of Kaitlyn over Lacey's shoulder. He tried to lock eyes with her, his stare falling short of some attempt at smoldering. Jonathan Wylie elicited an unrefined feeling of disgust in Kaitlyn. She would have liked to smack the ratty smile off his face with a manure fork. It would have been an improvement. Everything about his nature and appearance suggested he wasn't trustworthy. His mischievous brown eyes beneath eyebrows as thick as a caterpillar. His meticulous mustache. Even his proud walk was too much for Kaitlyn to stand, and he strode with a particular loftiness as he walked to the porch.

"Afternoon, ladies," Mr. Wylie said as he stepped up onto the white-painted wooden boards and leaned against the railing. He eyed the lemonade with a hinting glance that Lacey caught immediately.

"Oh! Where are my manners?" Lacey chirped. She reached for the pitcher of lemonade before realizing that she didn't have another glass. "I'll just run inside the house and fetch us another lemonade for you, Mr. Wylie," she said.

"Thank you kindly, dear," Wylie replied.

Lacey blushed a bright shade of pink.

Before Kaitlyn could protest, Lacey was gone, leaving her alone with Mr. Wylie on the porch.

It was difficult to avoid his gaze, and Kaitlyn felt her cheeks changing color- but in an irritated manner- as Wylie endowed his smile upon her. She racked her brain for a piece of small talk to say, but his eyes made it impossible to think. Wylie broke the silence soon enough.

"I've just picked up something you might have an appreciation for, Miss Heide," Wylie said. He reached a soft hand inside of the brown paper bag and pulled out a dazzling set of spurs. They were brilliant silver with an intricate pattern Kaitlyn couldn't quite make out engraved along the sides. Kaitlyn reached out unintentionally, drawn to the shimmering scene. When she realized what her hand had done, she tried to return it to her lap as quickly as possible, but Wylie had already seen her reaction. His smile turned into a laugh as he placed the spurs in Kaitlyn's hands.

"I had been bothering Bob to find me a custom pair for quite some time," he said. "It's so hard to find a man that can work with metal who isn't wasting his talent pounding on horseshoes. Then once you find the man, he's got a year-long waiting list, or he can't make the details just right and he still wants you to buy the pair that's all wrong just because he's already made them." Wylie explained all of this as though it was the most fascinating struggle in the world. "I seem to remember your brother who came down to sell cattle last year was a spur maker himself," he said.

It took a moment for Kaitlyn to piece together what Mr. Wylie had meant to say. Her brother had died a long time ago, but the only person in the crew who messed around with metal work was Garrett.

"Garret can make a good working set of spurs," Kaitlyn finally said. "He isn't my brother though," she added. "He's a friend that works for the family."

The mention of him made Kaitlyn wish that it was Garrett leaning against the porch rail shooting the breeze. She could have talked with him for hours and been a good deal more comfortable. If only she had one of her old companions for decent company in this town.

Living on the ranch miles and miles from town had never felt this lonely.

Just as the conversation was running out of steam, Lacey reappeared to pour a third glass of lemonade. She sat back in her chair and gushed to Wylie about her husband's job at the railroad yard and how happy they were to have it. Then she went on about other matters in the town while Kaitlyn smiled politely and desperately hoped that Lacey wouldn't leave again until the encounter was over.

Mr. Wylie remained leaning with his back to the street so that he was the last person to see the enormous plume of dust rising in the middle of the town.

The source of the dust was none other than the Wylie kids. Jud and Jeremiah had decided to race the main street on a busy Saturday at full gallop. Carriages and pedestrians already crowded the town, leaving only a very narrow strip between travelers going north and south. The brothers had chosen this sliver of road for their sprint. The stupidity of their race had undoubtedly occurred to even them, which made it all the more fun for young boys to try.

As their horses thundered past the general store, another figure became evident in the background. Behind them, Minnie was galloping full blast, her red ears pinned back flat against her head, while Darla clung to her like a kookaburra. The little blonde girl looked like a ragdoll clinging to the saddle horn with both hands — her reins were still tucked somewhere between her fingers, but they weren't doing her any good. Her horse raced on with the others despite her occasional desperate, "Woah."

The chaotic thudding of hooves was nearing the end of town, and for a moment Kaitlyn thought that everyone would escape the race unscathed. At that very second, for no reason that anyone could see, Minnie finally delivered on her pinned-ear promise to get rid of Darla. She planted her front feet into the ground, bouncing to a halt. Her hind feet came off the street a few inches in a crow-hop.

The miniature buck turned Darla's face a paler white but did nothing to unseat her. The mare snorted, pawing the ground angrily before she reared up, nearly sending her tiny rider off over the back of the saddle. Minnie returned to earth, shaking Darla's feet out of her stirrups. Somehow, the child still clung to the saddle horn while Minnie rose again. This time, the horse reared higher, wobbling on her extended back legs. Kaitlyn's throat tightened. She could see that the horse was going to fall over backward.

Kaitlyn rushed to the red roan. Dodging her striking front hooves, she tore the left rein out of Darla's hand and pulled the mare's head around to the side with all her might. Thrown off balance, the horse had no choice but to return to earth. Kaitlyn quickly delivered Darla to the safety of the ground. The young girl's trembling legs barely supported her as she hid behind the teacher's skirt.

"This is not a kid's horse!" Kaitlyn screamed. An evil spark still glowed in Minnie's eyes. "It's not a good horse at all!" she yelled. "Why would you breed for another one of these? It's not spirited; it's mean. It's just plain mean." Kaitlyn wasn't sure who she was yelling at, but she had never felt such a pure, shameless rage. She turned around, searching for Jonathan Wylie, ready to rip him to shreds but he wasn't there. He was in front of her, taking Minnie's reins.

The long-legged man swung onto the red mare, his brand new spurs shining like a diamond mine. Kaitlyn drug Darla back.

"Out of the way," she murmured.

Wylie took a tight hold of the reins and dug his spurs deep into the mare's sides. She pranced forward, swishing her tail in warning. He trotted the roan in a tight circle one way, then the other, then bullied her into a lope, all the while pulling the reins tighter. He finally stopped, satisfied with his work. His spurs left Minnie's side for just a moment with a drizzle of blood trickling off of them.

"Minnie is fine," he said. "Darla is just a poor rider."

Kaitlyn didn't need to argue. The words had barely left Wylie's mouth when the red mare reared back with all her might. She stretched her front hooves into the sky before toppling over backward. Minnie's back drove the saddle horn into the dirt with an awful crack. Wylie somehow wiggled himself to the side enough that only his foot was caught under the wreckage. Minnie, however, had proven that she was not a fine horse at all.

Chapter Four

The Heide Ranch corral was a rainbow of sorrel, grey, black, and buckskin colts. A good sized palomino filly even stood in the corner like a pot of gold at the rainbow's end. At the Boss's approach, five sets of ears swiveled forward curiously. The sorrel crept forward, nose outstretched until he stood with his face almost inside of John Heide's coat pocket.

"My wife has been giving you treats," the Boss muttered. He shooed the sorrel who wasn't the least bit offended but insisted on following him to inspect the rest of the herd.

The colts had wintered on the neighboring Deihl ranch that had more pasture and hadn't seen a person up close in several months. Aside from the sorrel, they glanced warily between the men.

"Garret, this pest is yours," the Boss announced, looking over his shoulder at the sorrel colt who was now sniffing his pants legs. "Work on him and the buckskin this week. Josh, you try out the grey and black ones. I'll start Goldie myself and hold her back as a broodmare if I like her."

The hired men nodded their acknowledgment. It was the Boss's habit to name the young horses once they were brought in to start under saddle. He believed there was something untrustworthy about a man that didn't name his horses.

"A man who won't treat his beast with some respect won't treat you any better," he claimed; and that adage had always proven true for him.

Their boots already caked with mud, Josh and Garrett waded forward. Each caught one horse and led them into the towering wooden barn. A thirty-foot space had been cleared inside. Palates had been used to round off the building's corners, making a lopsided round pen. With a tall grey filly's lead rope draped over his arm, Josh went about collecting various supplies stashed in an unused barn stall.

Meanwhile, Garret turned his sorrel loose in the makeshift pen, guiding him to trot along the perimeter until he began watching his new trainer closely, awaiting directions. When the young horse was paying attention well, Garrett let him rest and haltered him again.

Standing by the side of the improvised round pen, Garret reached out for Josh to pass him an empty feed sack. As he did so, the sorrel wiggled his nose into Garret's pocket and clamped his teeth down on a leftover dinner mint. Unfortunately, his wide bite caught a good chunk of fabric and skin with it.

"Get out of my pocket!" Garret yelped. He swatted at the gelding with the feed sack in his free hand, barely forcing the horse to retreat a few steps. The horse stared innocently, chewing on his hard stolen mint.

With a glare on his face, Garret shook the feed sack violently, making enough rustling noise to startle any unbroken horse. The gelding paused his chewing for a moment, eyed the bag with interest, and stepped forward in search of more food.

Josh's grey filly, on the other hand, shot backward at the sound of the bag. In the process, she ripped free of his hold. He scrambled to pick up the lead rope and glared at Garret's turned back.

"Take it easy!" Josh shouted. "At least warn a feller when you're going to do that."

"Are you sure this horse isn't already broke? He seems like a spoiled pet," Garret remarked.

"He's the one Mrs. Deihl had to keep in the barn to doctor. I remember the Boss saying he got a nasty wire cut. That must be why he's so, well, used to people."

"He's too used to being treated like a lap dog." Garrett had given up on the sack and stood rubbing his side where he had been bitten.

"At least he's easy to catch. It's better than having them be too wild."

"I'm sure he looks great when you're not the one who's got a chunk of your stomach missing."

Josh opened his mouth to reply with the first joke that came to mind but thought better of it. "He sure is in your pocket. I'll give you that."

From that point on, Garret took to calling the sorrel gelding Pocket. No one was ever quite sure if Pocket liked Garret or if he just harbored secret hope for more dinner mints. Either way, he was always the first horse at the gate, ready to be caught. Garret's buckskin, which he named Missy Lew, was never very far behind.

The grey filly, Pepper, proved to be trainable and willing. She had big soft eyes, and her lean build was a perfect match for

Josh's. He had to be on his toes with the black filly though. A close cousin to the mare the Boss had sent with Kaitlyn, she didn't exactly have a temper, but she was very sensitive. It was difficult to find a balance between gaining her respect and preserving her responsiveness.

Finding an appropriate title for her also proved challenging. Josh tried Raven, Beauty, then Blackie but none of them stuck.

The time passed methodically. Garret and Josh used the make-shift round pen in turns while the other watched. The ranch hands sacked the horses out with feed sacks, ropes, old Navajo blankets, and whatever else was handy; moving the foreign object at each colt until they cocked a hind foot or licked their lips in acceptance. It wasn't always easy, but once a horse was worked through the process of being desensitized to something new, he understood it wouldn't cause any harm and was no longer afraid of it.

On the third day, Garret carried a sturdy saddle into the barn with him. The veteran leather showed scuff marks but was freshly polished and stout. Each colt took their turn carrying it. Some stood calmly and trotted off without showing any concern, others crow hopped at the feeling of the cinch around their bellies.

Unsure what to do under pressure, Pepper reared straight towards the barn rafters. Her front hooves pawed the air; back legs stretched out to their full extent. For a moment, it looked as though she would tip over backward. Josh quickly pulled sideways on the lead rope, bringing her back to earth. Before she could rise again, he urged her forward firmly. Josh privately prayed she wouldn't attempt the same show when he rode her.

Thankfully, Pepper didn't offer to misbehave when the day came to start riding. Neither did Pocket, Missy Lew, or even Goldie.

Though the Boss tended to work alone, he joined his hired men for the day. His superior experience was evident. Goldie trotted around the pen with little urging. When she went into a lope, the Boss allowed her a lap to find her balance under the new weight of a rider before he sat down deep in the saddle and brought her to a stop. A newcomer to the scene could have mistaken Goldie for a well-broke horse.

Only the no-name black filly attempted to buck on her first ride. Josh had barely elicited two steps from the horse before her head shot into the air. All four legs followed in a blind frenzy. A horrible squeal escaped the mare as she returned to earth. Another massive heave followed. The black twisted in midair, snaking her neck out. She quickly unseated Josh, who had the bad fortune to land squarely on his tailbone.

The foreman regained his feet. Without bothering to shake away the dirt clinging to his pants, he grabbed ahold of the reins and worked the black from the ground until she was breathing heavily. When he tried to climb aboard for the second time, the horse began to buck and skitter sideways while he still had only one boot in the stirrup.

This time, Josh slid from the saddle of his own accord, his eyes laced with adrenaline. He managed to keep ahold of the reins; his fist clenched so tightly that his fingers began to turn white. The filly found the limit of the round pen and pulled away. With no regard for the man on the ground, she twisted around, ripping free. Her tail end knocked into Josh, and she ran a victory lap while he regained his balance.

Once the horse had stepped on the loose reins that ran along beneath her, she stopped, confused. She stared at Josh as if she believed she had been caught. Josh took his chance. He grabbed ahold of the wild filly firmly. His mind replayed her jumps, planning a way to counter them from the saddle. He was about to spring for the stirrup again, but he was interrupted.

"Put her up," the Boss ordered. "She's not ready."

Josh's heart still pounded. His head was cloudy. Even his fingertips trembled as he undid the saddle and slid it off. Sweat soaked his sleeves, but the black horse was hardly wet. She didn't try any more tricks and based on her expression she didn't seem to know she'd done anything out of the ordinary. Josh sulked back to the corral, leading his nameless bronco. His pride stung.

The Boss followed not far behind. He hesitated for a moment, then called Josh aside.

"I can buck her out," Josh insisted. "I just need another try," Josh insisted.

"That's beside the point," the Boss replied quietly. "I used to do it that way when I was younger. We ruined some good horses bucking them out. They never settle down, and they never trust you. When I got old enough that I didn't want to break any more bones, I went back and learned a better way to do it, and that's what I want to have done on my operation."

Josh stared down at the dirt on his boots.

"You're doing a really nice job with the grey horse," the Boss continued. "The black one will come along too. It's nothing you're doing wrong. Some horses just take longer."

The Boss left Josh alone with that thought resounding in his head. The foreman leaned back against the corral fence and watched the horses picking at a feeder full of hay. His mind had cleared from a frantic mania to simple misery. He wasn't granted much time alone with his thoughts. Garret soon appeared bareback on Pocket, whom he'd only ridden twice to date.

"How's your tail?" Garret laughed. "She sure had something to say about being a saddle horse!" Garret reached down and patted his colt on the neck. He didn't have much control over Pocket yet, but it was a sure bet that a young horse would go back to his herd if given a choice. Since that was where Garret had wanted to go anyway, it gave the illusion that he was steering the horse underneath him.

Frustration boiled inside Josh's head. He contemplated punching Garret's smug grin, but his fist stayed clenched against his leg. Fighting the black horse hadn't done him any good, and with the way his luck was going, he wasn't about to start a brand new fight. He turned to walk back to the bunkhouse.

Garret put his horse up quickly and fell into step. When he saw Josh's face, Garret stopped laughing.

"Even the best bronc riders on earth only have to stay on for eight seconds," Garret offered. "I'd say you were up there for at least six."

"A horse can keep bucking a whole lot longer than that," the Boss called. Neither of the hands had noticed him going about Dorothy's usual chores. The sturdy man looked odd carrying an apron-full of fragile chicken eggs.

Josh didn't care to talk to him, or to anyone for that matter. Luckily, the Boss didn't have anything else to say. Josh made a peaceful escape to the confines of the bunkhouse. He peeled off his dust-covered clothes, ran a wet towel over his face, and climbed under the quilt on his bed without saying a word. His face was still twisted in frustration. He lay back and closed his eyes, wishing the day's fiasco had been nothing but a dream.

Since the weather had warmed up, the ranch hands had been able to do most of their cooking inside the bunkhouse. Garret, whose cooking skills had improved slightly, got the cook stove going and threw a slab of bacon in the frying pan.

Not one to keep quiet for too long, Garrett finally broke the silence.

"Holding a grudge is a sin, brother," Garret said.

Josh laughed sarcastically. "Even against a horse?" he replied.

"I'd say you're still the one suffering from being so darn mad over just one bad day."

"Just one bad day?" Josh sat up in protest. "It wasn't just any bad day. It was the first ride. I did something wrong. I missed something, but I don't know what."

"Well, you don't have to get it right every single time," Garret said.

"That's easy to say if you've got all the easy horses and being wrong doesn't get you bucked off," Josh snapped.

Garret's jaw tightened. It wasn't very often that Josh got worked up and it was hard to decide how to handle it. The bacon simmering was the only sound in the room for a few moments.

"If you want me to, I can show you what I would do with the black horse," Garret said in a tone that gave away the fact he was trying too hard not to catch Josh's bad mood. "I'm not saying it's the only way, but it's what I would do."

Josh slid back down onto his pillow. "Look, I don't mean to bite your hand, but I've been doing this twice as long as you have. How is it that you know all this little stuff that I haven't ever heard of?"

"I talk to Mrs. Heide," Garret replied. "Her daddy was a horseman that had all girls. I think she might know more about young horses than the Boss does and she's a lot easier to ask questions."

Too tired and sore to concern himself with eating dinner, Josh closed his eyes again. He silently envisioned loping the pretty black mare and decided he would accept Garret's offer in the morning. If it worked, he would be one step closer to having a broke horse.

The next morning found Josh poised on top of a heavy wooden crate, sliding his left leg up and down on his black mare's back. She was haltered but unsaddled, her dark coat the color of late night. Josh felt ridiculous, but he figured that Garret's idea was worth a shot.

"Why am I doing this?" He muttered under his breath.

Garret, who was standing in the center of the round pen, caught the comment. "It'll work. That's why," Garret said.

The foreman continued rubbing his leg against the mare. His pants were steadily collecting horsehair. He didn't mind though. It was preferable to the dust bath he'd gotten the day before. Though he would have never admitted it, every instinct in his body was trying to keep him from getting back on the black horse. He would have rather climbed on any other horse, even one that he knew was going to buck. It was not knowing what would happen that bothered him.

Trying to relax, Josh leaned over the mare's back, resting his elbows on her withers. Her head shot up immediately, eyes wide in alarm. She backed up quickly, forcing Josh to jump up out of the way to avoid having his head hit.

"There! That's your problem!" Garret yelled excitedly. "She doesn't like seeing you out of both eyes. It's not normal for her."

"Great," Josh said sarcastically. He wasn't sure why Garret was so enthused about a problem that didn't seem to make any sense. "So what do you want me to do, ride her side saddle for the rest of her life?" he added.

"Yes, that's the only thing to do," Garret joked. "Actually, if you just keep leaning over her there and petting on her, it should do her some good," he said in a more serious tone.

It took Josh a few minutes to reposition his horse and lean over her withers again. Once more, the mare threw her head up, nostrils flaring but it was a moment more before she started moving away. Josh tried again and again. On the fourth attempt, the mare seemed to slow down and think about how things were playing out. Her feet remained still as her ears swiveled back towards Josh and forward to Garret.

"See if I were to snub her up or ear her, you'd be able to get on that one time, but it would be a long road from there to you ever being able to get on her again without having her restrained like that," Garret started preaching. "Teach her to let you get on from the start, and it won't ever be a big deal."

Josh was doing his best to pretend he wasn't as tense as a seller at a cattle auction. He knew he needed to be calm for this to work but the harder he tried to relax, the tenser he seemed to make himself. Forcing his mouth into a slight smile, he tried to unwind his nerves. He rubbed his long, calloused fingers over the mare's black mane, talking to her quietly. She stood blinking slowly and exhaled, her muscles relaxing.

Garret nodded his approval. "Now you can go ahead and put some weight on her. Just lean over some more but keep both your legs off to this left side."

Josh felt more confident than he had even a minute ago. Still, he knew what to expect when he put all his weight on the sensitive mare's back. She moved sideways like a lightning bolt. Josh kept a handful of mane and did his best to hold on, hanging over the side of the horse like a stuntman, until she came to a stop. He was glad to hop down. Returning to the wooden crate, he repeated the whole process three more times until the horse would let him wiggle all over her back without flinching.

Finally, the moment came to see if Garret's method had worked. Josh slowly moved his right leg into position, straddling his horse, and sat up straight. He waited apprehensively, taking forced breaths. The lanky rider was pretending to be calm for his horse's sake and he could only hope she wouldn't call his bluff.

The black mare turned her head back to sniff at Josh's boot, then drowsily cocked a hind foot. Josh grinned. He used the lead rope he'd made into reins to guide her a few steps in small circles. She walked forward without protest, but Josh brought her head around to stop her before she could change her mind about behaving.

Garret chuckled, "Now you just have to do that a thousand more times, and you'll have yourself a broke horse."

Chapter Five

The school day ended with its usual flair. Kaitlyn moseyed about the schoolhouse straightening out the rows of desks and dusting books off. She found a few new inscriptions carved underneath Jeremiah Wylie's desks. Thankfully they were only initials and nothing too creative. The desk that served as Jeremiah's footstool suffered the worst wear. He'd carved a deep letter W into it, probably using his spur.

The schoolteacher moved on to dusting the windows just in time to catch sight of Mr. Wylie approaching the schoolhouse. Her cheeks flushed. Wylie's injured leg was bound up in a solid cast, so he made slow progress. Kaitlyn darted away from the window before he could see her.

After the incident with the red roan, Darla had been coming to school on a twenty-six-year-old sporting pony that had three legs in the grave. Kaitlyn hadn't seen Mr. Wylie since he'd crawled out from underneath the red horse and been rushed off to the doctor. The rumor around town was that he'd be having a little talk with the schoolteacher once he was back on his feet. Kaitlyn could only imagine and dread what that talk would entail. The receiving end of the business man's anger was not a good place to be.

A knock came at the door. For a moment, Kaitlyn thought about pretending nobody was home. She figured she could sit down at a desk and be out of sight until he went away. On the other hand, the confrontation had to come sooner or later. Kaitlyn reluctantly opened the door.

Wylie stood by the old dinner bell, leaning on his crutches. His mustache was neatly groomed, and he appeared to be starting a beard to match it.

"Miss Kaitlyn," he said, hat in hand, "I've come to see if you will accompany me to dinner."

Kaitlyn's jaw nearly dropped. "Why?" The word escaped her unintentionally.

Mr. Wylie chuckled. "How does the Longhorn at six suit you? You are free this evening, aren't you?"

Unsure what to say, Kaitlyn nodded. She repeated his offer. "Longhorn at Six." Kaitlyn was only trying to wrap her mind around the proposition, but she realized too late that her words had been taken as an acceptance.

"Very good. I'll see you then," Wylie said. He turned to go, and Kaitlyn watched him hobble down the road, dreading what she'd gotten herself into now.

With only one way she could clear her head, Kaitlyn quickly saddled Dolly and tore off into the wind. Sitting in her small pen at the school all day made the mare frisky. She had extra prance to her step and held her tail high in the air like an Arabian. It took all of Kaitlyn's considerable skill to keep Dolly from going into a full gallop until they were clear of town. She wanted to run from Mr. Wylie, but she didn't want to start any gossip about it. A woman who galloped out of town as fast as she could in response to the railroad owner's dinner invitation would no doubt be dubbed as crazy.

As soon as she was sure they were out of sight, Kaitlyn gave Dolly a longer rein and pushed her into a sprinting gallop. The black mare streaked across the flat land towards the hills. Wind battered Kaitlyn's ears. She held a hand up to shield at least one of them from its howling.

Kaitlyn looked out to the distant mountains that she could race towards but never reach. Framed between Dolly's black ears, the grass whipped violently in the afternoon windstorm. She brought Dolly down to a walk and allowed her a few minutes to catch her breath. The wind had already carried any traces of sweat away from her bright coat.

"I have a date tonight," Kaitlyn said, half to Dolly and half to herself. The black mare's ears flicked back towards the rider's voice. "I'm not going. We'll just run away instead," she mused.

The wind was becoming too much to bear. Kaitlyn steered Dolly into a shallow glen and dismounted. The second that she was free of her rider, Dolly's head shot down into the grass. Kaitlyn found a downed tree to rest her back against and sat there while the minutes rolled past.

It was quiet in the gully. Kaitlyn could hear herself think. She sat back and closed her eyes. Breathing deeply, the young woman listened for the sound of Dolly's chewing to reassure her the horse was still there. She prayed for a few minutes, but she wasn't sure what she was praying for, so she let her mind go blank. Soon, she drifted into her memories...

It had been one of the mildest winters on record, not that there was much of a record to go by. A gentle blanket of snow enveloped the ground underneath a clear sky. Grandpa Heide and the neighbor, Mr. Deihl, agreed they had never had such a pleasant winter.

Kaitlyn sat, legs crisscrossed, on the living room floor with a heavy quilted blanket covering her lap. Grandma Heide inhabited the wicker chair behind her. The gentle old woman hummed while she twisted Kaitlyn's blonde hair into a complicated updo. It was tradition for the ladies on the ranch to spend Saturday mornings fixing each other's hair just to see what they could come up with. Grandma Heide slipped one last pin into her granddaughter's fresh curls and announced she was done.

She was just about to race for the mirror in her room when Kaitlyn heard the door swung open. A parade of heavy boots trudged across the floor. Grandpa Heide appeared, two inches of snow still resting on top of his boots. More white powder was clinging to his pant legs and the longer he stood there, the more it puddled up on the floor.

"My rug!" Grandma Heide cried.

Grandpa looked down at his boots like he hadn't noticed he was wearing them. He shrugged. He was grinning boyishly and his face was bright red from the cold. Before he could speak, his wife repeated her complaint.

"What makes you think you need to be in the living room with those boots on? Look at that muddy snow!"

"Now, easy," Grandpa said. His eyes had a mischievous look to them. He turned his attention to Kaitlyn. "I have a surprise for you."

She leaned forward, intrigued. The blonde checked the pins in her hair quickly to make sure they would hold if she moved. She rose to her feet just as Garret poked his head into the room.

"Are you going someplace?" he asked. Garret had been much scrawnier back then. He looked a bit like a colt who hadn't filled out enough for his height. His dark brown hair was too thick to possibly tame. It stuck out like a rooster tail in back and didn't behave much better on the sides either. Only his dark green eyes resembled the man he would shortly grow into.

Kaitlyn scowled at him. Of course appreciating a little sophistication was beyond the ranch hands. Garret didn't get a response from Kaitlyn. Instead, Grandpa Heide answered.

"She's going to the barn to see her surprise." He turned to leave. "Are you coming Dorothy?" he asked. The rancher's wife had her lips pressed together tightly. Without a word, she took a large rag out of the corner and handed it to her husband.

"Oh," Grandpa muttered. "All right." He bent down to grab the chunks of snow off the floor. Dorothy's glare lessened.

"What's so all important in the barn?" she asked.

Garret opened his mouth to answer. The Boss quickly smashed a handful of snow over the boy's face.

"Don't spoil it!" the Boss warned.

Everyone chuckled while Garret shook the snow off his stunned face. The Boss elbowed him jokingly and Garret began to laugh too.

"Girls, come see for yourselves," Grandpa said. With his towel full of snow in hand, he walked to the door and out into the cold. Kaitlyn eyed her grandmother. Both women slipped their coats on simultaneously and followed, giggling more like sisters than women born two generations apart.

It took all of Garret's strength at the time to open the barn doors against the snow drifts. When he managed to, the smell of pine trees gushed inside and mixed with the aroma of rich hay.

A tiny foal sat in the great barn. Her wide brown eyes stared inquisitively at the straw she'd fallen into. She was jet black, so new to the world that her coat was still wet. A white star graced her forehead.

As the small crowd gathered around the edges of the barn, the foal decided to try testing her feet. The black's wobbly knees rose out of the bedding, displaying bright white socks. She spread her front legs wide and stumbled, trying to stand up. When at last she succeeded, her back legs matched the front.

Suddenly, Kaitlyn's breath caught in her throat. She was old enough to know how to be sensible but she just couldn't help falling in love at first sight. All of her life she'd waited for a horse of her own to come along. Not a horse that was Grandpa's first and hers second. Not a ranch worker's old hand-me-down. A horse that was her very own in every way. This felt like the moment she'd been waiting for.

"She's got some fancy markings!" Grandma Heide exclaimed.

Kaitlyn was beaming. "She couldn't be more perfect if she were a doll."

The newborn filly took a cautious step towards her mother. She must have wanted to get back to something familiar amidst all the new faces.

The foal's dam, Tillie, was a gentle old soul. Back in those days, the Heide's had kept a stallion of their own named Prophet. The problem was that Prophet could be very crafty about getting out of his pen to visit the mares on his own schedule. It was one such escape that resulted in Tillie being accidentally bred at age twenty-two.

Though she was old to be a mother, Tillie was in excellent shape. She was perfectly plump and her dark coat was plush. She was content nursing her new baby. The symmetrically marked filly took a long time drinking before she emerged with a white foam of milk covering her muzzle.

"She's got a healthy appetite," Garret observed. The filly's ears tipped towards the sound of his voice. She began to wobble forward towards her visitors. She stopped five feet away from Garret and suddenly seemed to change her mind. Her feeble black legs darted back to the safety of her mother, nearly collapsing in the process. It was a wonderful sight to see her tiny white socks dancing clumsily in the straw.

If she'd thought she could hide behind Tillie, the foal was mistaken. The old mare sat down to rest, leaving her baby in full view of the crowd. With the strangers staring at her, the black filly made one more trip to investigate. Her steps grew slower and less calculated as she moved. By the time the newborn horse reached her destination, she'd run out of energy to keep going. She sunk to the ground in front of Kaitlyn, almost on top of the girl's dress. Her brown eyes blinked drowsily.

"I think she's chosen you," Grandpa laughed.

"Hi little doll," Kaitlyn said. She reached down to touch the foal's black fur. It was the softest thing she'd ever felt. "You really are as perfect as a doll," she crooned. "I think I'll call you Dolly."

Unable to hide her excitement, Kaitlyn rushed to the barn every morning for the next two weeks. Dolly's tiny nicker grew in increments. The filly was strong and lanky like Prophet but her markings were all her own. Kaitlyn watched Dolly tear around the barn, often running between Tillie's legs. The rancher's granddaughter always gave the sweet old broodmare an apple from the root cellar to eat while she groomed Dolly's white socks.

With the warm weather still holding up, Grandpa determined that Dolly was old enough for the pair to move to an outside paddock. It was news to Dolly that she and her mother were not the only horses in the world. The other broodmares, who would not be having their babies until April, largely ignored her squealing as she bounced between them.

The filly had never seen so much room to run. Her short black tail cracked like a whip whenever she changed directions in her imaginary race. Occasionally, Tillie humored her baby, trotting along the fence line beside her.

The paddock was in full view from Kaitlyn's bedroom window. As the weeks passed, she fell into the habit of ignoring her school books to watch Dolly and Tillie play. She thought to herself that she'd never seen a more perfect relationship between a mother and her foal.

One morning, not long after Dolly was born, Kaitlyn had been on a rare trip to town. Not trusting him to do the job, she'd accompanied Garret to pick out new clothes for the church social. When she got home, Grandma Heide took her aside and explained Tillie had suddenly had a fit of colic. They had tried everything including an old remedy of whiskey, coffee, and cooking oil but it had done no good. Kaitlyn was too stunned to know how to respond. Death was a part of life on the ranch but Tillie had been so healthy just the day before.

Grandpa Heide locked Dolly up in the barn and tried to get her to drink milk from a bottle but she wouldn't take it. He suggested Kaitlyn go see the foal, hoping it would cheer her up. On her way across the snowy yard, Kaitlyn ran into Garret.

"I'm so sorry about Tillie," he said immediately. His cheeks were flushed. He looked sweaty and flustered.

"I'm sorry too," Kaitlyn managed.

"Wasn't that your mom's horse?"

"Yes," Kaitlyn replied quietly.

"Oh, um, you're handling it well," Garret stammered. "You've always been a strong one though."

"Thanks," Kaitlyn whispered. Her voice barely came out. She turned to go.

She opened a crack in the barn door just wide enough to slip through. Once inside, she leaned against the closed door. Kaitlyn sobbed. She felt like she'd become too accustomed to losing animals, and maybe people too. If one more person told her she was being strong, she didn't think she could handle it.

Kaitlyn's blue eyes locked on the little black filly. She'd given up looking for her mother and stood with her head drooped to the straw. Dolly's gaze met with the young woman's. She gave a tiny nicker. The foal's voice was hoarse from calling out for Tillie. Kaitlyn rushed forward and knelt beside the filly, wrapping her arms around her.

She patted Dolly's slender black neck.

"I know," Kaitlyn whispered. "Trust me, Dolly, I know it's hard to lose your mama when you're so young." The foal looked up expectantly and nuzzled Kaitlyn's coat, looking for milk. It was impossible not to smile. "You'll be okay, though," Kaitlyn said. "I'll take good care of you."

With new resolve, Kaitlyn ran into the ranch house and placed a pot of water on the stove. She grabbed the milk bottle Grandpa had tried earlier and quickly dumped its contents outside. Filling the bottle with fresh milk, Kaitlyn warmed it on the stove. She tested the temperature of the milk on her wrist several times before it was just a little too hot. It would cool enough to be palatable by the time she got out to the barn.

It was wishful thinking to assume the filly would drink from a bottle easily. Kaitlyn tried everything she could imagine to coax Dolly, but her black muzzle twisted away from the milk bottle at every chance. Desperate, Kaitlyn finally squeezed the now lukewarm milk onto her fingertips. She held her hand to Dolly's nose. Recognition lit up the filly's eyes. Her tiny pink tongue tested the unfamiliar milk.

Kaitlyn's hands were terribly sticky by the time Dolly had gotten any food in her stomach. Each time she cupped her hands together, the foal would take what milk could fit in her palms but no amount of trying could convince Dolly that a bottle could be trusted.

Watching Dolly lap up her dinner eventually gave Kaitlyn an idea. She found a shallow feed pan and dumped the remaining half bottle of milk into it. The ranch girl settled into the clean straw, her back against the stall wall. She offered the bowl to Dolly, pushing it close to her nose.

The wary foal sniffed suspiciously. Finally, she took a long, steady drink. Though she didn't finish the bowl, she finally understood it was milk. Dolly's brown eyes showed relief on either side of her white star.

It was evening when Kaitlyn realized she'd been dozing in the straw. Garret's footsteps woke her but she didn't move. She saw that the filly was sitting contently, eyes barely open. Kaitlyn closed her own eyes again as Garret awkwardly draped his wool coat around her shoulders. His hands were surprisingly strong.

With her eyes closed tightly, Kaitlyn almost felt like she could be back in the barn once again. She dwelled on the meaning of Garret's gesture. The young woman missed him deeply. She missed every part of her home.

Missing something wouldn't bring it back though. There was only today, and today, the Dillon evening arrived too soon. Kaitlyn hadn't meant for it to happen, but she found herself dressed in a pink dress she seldom wore, preparing to meet Mr. Wylie.

Her fingers flew down her blonde hair, twisting sections into two braids. She tied the braids off. A simple pair of black shoes waited by the door. She slipped them on and hurried outside before she could think better of it.

The Longhorn was a cafe, a saloon, a fine dining establishment, and whatever else a customer might want it to be. Silver candle holders graced the tables from six p.m. until nine p.m. or so. Afterward, the heavy drinking, card playing crowd would show up and stay until closing time, which was very loosely enforced. In the morning, the waitresses would set up to serve casual breakfast and lunch menus. Once six p.m. rolled around, the fine tablecloths came out, and the cycle started all over again.

Kaitlyn stood in the entryway, letting her eyes adjust to the Longhorn's dim light. A young woman walked in behind her, escorted from home by her gentleman caller. It occurred to Kaitlyn that Wylie should have done the same for her. It was too late to worry about that now.

Tall mirrors hung in the Longhorn's entrance. Kaitlyn stared into one, wondering if it would give her a better perspective on herself. A foggy reflection of her blue eyes gazed back. Neither the real Kaitlyn nor the mirrored one knew what to think.

She had been standing there for a few minutes, gaining nervousness, when a scraggly young man in a waiter's uniform approached her.

"Are you meeting J.B.?" he said.

"Excuse me, what was that?" she asked, confused.

"J.B. Wylie party of two has a reservation at six," the waiter explained.

"Oh, yes," Kaitlyn replied. "I'm meeting, um, Mr. Wylie."

The waiter led her through the dining room to a quiet table in the back. Wylie was seated behind a tall bouquet, sipping coffee. When Kaitlyn sat down, he moved the flowers off to the side. He greeted her with a smile. His eyes didn't look as detestable as they had before.

"Do people call you J.B.?" Kaitlyn asked.

"Sometimes. Jonathan Beauford is a mouthful," he replied. "Jonathan was my father's name. It was his father's name also. There can only be so many men named Jon or Jonathan in one family."

"You didn't go for Johnny?" Kaitlyn asked. She wasn't comfortable joking with Wylie, but it was the only thing she could think to say.

"No," he replied. He reached out to pour a glass of water from the pitcher on the table.

Kaitlyn nodded her head. She spent as much time distracted by her menu as she could until the waiter came back with an order notepad. Though he was probably around fourteen, Kaitlyn had never seen the boy in school before. His eyes were a dark green, the darkest green she'd ever seen, except for maybe Garret's.

"Prime rib steak, medium well-done," she told the waiter. As long as Wylie was paying for dinner, she might as well order something expensive.

"A woman of fine taste," the boy commented.

"I know what I like," she replied with a smile.

"And how do you like being the teacher in Dillon?" Wylie asked.

Kaitlyn took a long drink, nibbling one of the ice cubes that had floated to the top. "It's fine," she finally replied.

Wylie didn't seem honestly interested in the subject. He preferred to talk about his cattle operation, his railroad business, anything to do with himself. Kaitlyn could tell when he didn't know what he was talking about, but she managed to bite her tongue. She ate slowly, giving Wylie a chance to run the conversation while she chewed. She made it through dinner and dessert in this manner.

By the end of the evening, Kaitlyn almost believed J.B. Wylie could be everything he said he was. His talk was very compelling, but then again, he'd lied to her before. The fact that her date had made her meet him in town instead of picking her up at the schoolhouse was still bothering her as she stood to leave. With all his money, he still had no idea how to be a gentleman.

"Would you walk me home?" she asked.

A crooked smile tilted Wylie's mustache off center. He offered Kaitlyn his arm. "Why, of course," he replied. "I'll make sure you get home."

Chapter Six

Beams of sunlight warmed Josh's face and arms. He'd rolled his shirt sleeves up enough to soak in the sunshine where his skin hadn't seen any in months. It always seemed like true summer would never come in Montana. The spring was a cruel joke that drifted between snow and rain, thawing days and freezing nights. Looking around at the sunbathing cattle, who loved the new weather just as much as the cowboys did, Josh decided that summer was finally here to stay.

Dorothy's strength had returned just as the early flowers began to bloom in her garden. Tall lavender stems stretched heavenward. Stocky little marigolds danced around patches of white daisies and bright yellow snapdragons. Life was renewed again. Even along the county road, God had done some gardening of his own, planting a mix of tiny bluebells and great sunflowers to brighten the world.

John Heide was more than ready to have his lifelong companion back to her usual self.

Garret's questionable cooking was replaced by hearty breakfasts, pie with noontime dinner, and suppers that drew the men inside almost before the day's work was done. Dorothy also lent herself to lighter outdoor work, tending flowers and gathering eggs from the chickens and ducks.

When the midday temperatures climbed, Dorothy could be found sitting on the porch swing. She poured over breeding records, marking down the ear tag numbers of heifers that would be sold off. Occasionally, she raised her blue eyes from the leather-bound record book and tucked a loose lock of black hair back into the long braid that hung down her back; and John thought she had never looked more beautiful.

With the new temperature came a whole new line of work on the Heide Ranch. Gates to the upper mountain pastures would be opened for the first time since late October. Bushels of dryland grass had gotten a healthy head start from the snowmelt. Cattle who had been around for a few summers looked over the low hills in anticipation. They knew the routine.

Once the first set of gates opened, they would stay in the vast, "middle pastures," as Garret called them, until a dent had been made in the available forage. It was a trick of strategically placing salt blocks that cattle craved far enough away from water sources to make sure that they didn't overgraze any one area of the pasture or neglect others.

The Heide Ranch's burro, Tater, would trail along behind the other animals, eating down any weeds the horses and cows might not have had an interest in devouring. Garrett had won ownership of Tater by accident. A few years earlier, he had fancied himself a pretty good farrier and started putting up ads to make an extra dollar. The first three men to call on Garrett's farrier services all had horses that nearly kicked his head off.

The fourth customer had a string of half a dozen horses that were very well behaved. To Garret's relief, he was able to put on six sets of shoes without any fussing. It was only after the last nail was pounded in that Garret found out the man didn't have any money to pay with. What the man did have was a burro. Garret found Tater to be a good companion, but he didn't shoe other people's horses anymore.

Tater wasn't worth the price of six sets of shoes, but Garret got a laugh out of petting the little burro when he checked the cattle and went to open the next set of gates. In the hottest part of summer, when there was enough grass in the pine trees at the very top of the mountain to sustain a few weeks of grazing, the crew again opened a few gates and pushed the cattle up to higher elevation.

There were known to be black bears and the occasional mountain lion in the top section of the mountain. These usually didn't bother cattle, preferring to go after deer which were much smaller and easier prey. It was only when signs of timber wolves appeared that the Boss got nervous.

Some years ago, a city man named Reeves had purchased timber wolves from a drunkard in Canada, thinking they would make beautiful sled dogs. How the Canadian had managed to live trap and transport a dozen timber wolves was the subject of many tall tales. Of course, the animals were not dogs. When it had reached a certain age, the largest wolf decided he might like to be the alpha and promptly killed Reeves. Ten of the twelve wolves managed to escape their bondage. The other two became an excellent winter coat auctioned off to benefit Reeve's widow who had stayed back East.

The wolves didn't fit in too well. The pack multiplied to nearly twenty the first winter they ran loose. They were immigrants to Montana and didn't receive a warm welcome from ranchers or other wildlife. Wolves were the only animal that killed solely for sport rather than meat; and unlike the smaller grey wolves that had been native to the territory, these timber wolves managed to do a great deal of livestock massacring very quickly.

There was still a small, high-end market for furs but it had been many decades since trapping was a common trade. John Heide and Edward Deihl had searched several counties to find a trapper they could commission since neither had the extra time to check a trap line. When a trapper from near Helena took the job, they were more than happy at just the thought of being rid of the non-native wolves.

If the Boss didn't have time to check a trap line, he certainly didn't have time to make the annual spring cattle drive, taking extra heifers to market. Both Josh and Garret hoped and prayed the Boss would hire them extra help for the journey. Yearling heifers were not among God's smartest creation. Keeping them together and all headed in one direction tended to wear out everybody involved, including the cattle themselves.

The Boss knew it was unrealistic to expect the two men to go so far without losing cattle. If it came down to it, he reasoned he could post an advertisement at the feed store in Helena. That could be risky though. Helena was a mining settlement and offering work to just anyone from there could bring in some unsavory characters.

The Heide's paid good wages which had its pros and cons. It inspired just about everyone who had ever worked for them to put in long hard days without growing bitter. It also allowed the workers with foresight to put a little aside every month until they had enough saved up to buy a small piece of land

and strike out on their own. The Boss was glad to see people succeed, but he sometimes missed having the help of former ranch hands. He half wished a few of them would come miraculously riding down the driveway to help with the spring cattle drive.

Unfortunately, none of the old seasonal help had written looking for work this year. It was for this reason that nobody thought it would be the answer to their problems when three unfamiliar figures came riding up the road towards the homestead. The Boss and Josh were occupied sorting the sale heifers out from the rest of the herd and wouldn't have been bothered to stop their work even if they had noticed someone was arriving.

Garrett looked up just long enough to drip red paint from the fence he'd been touching up. He placed the lid back on his paint can and sat the paintbrush down on top of it. There were a few sections of fence left to do, but they could wait. He strode towards the unfamiliar riders, his tall, broad figure casting a wide shadow on the ground in front of him.

The ranch hand met the three riders in the middle of the ranch yard, just in front of the main house. He looked the newcomers over, trying not to look too unfriendly but secretly suspicious of folks he'd never seen before showing up unannounced.

"What can I do for you boys?" Garrett asked.

It was the man riding in the middle and slightly ahead of the other two who answered.

"We're looking for John Heide," he replied. "Are you him?"

"No, sir. He's out in the corrals."

"Edward Deihl sent us this way," the stranger continued. "He said your group needed some help taking cows south to market. We're heading south anyway, and we wouldn't mind a few extra dollars to help with the journey. How much does the job pay?"

"Well, you'd have to talk to the Boss about that." Garret paused, wishing that the men would get down from their horses so that they could talk at eye level. He was not keen on having to look up so far to look a man in the eyes. When none of the riders moved or spoke, he decided to continue.

"If you want to talk with him about hiring on, he'll be in for supper in an hour or so. I can show you all where to water your horses," Garret offered.

"We'd be much obliged," the rider in the middle returned.

Garret walked them to the horse's stock tank where they finally dismounted. Their horses drank greedily, visibly sucking the water level down. The man who had spoken for the group offered a stiff handshake and introduced himself as William Hofstede.

William Hofstede had a thinly trimmed brown mustache with a bare splotch in the middle. Every time Garret looked at him, he wished he would shave it. He seemed pleasant enough otherwise. He wore a fringed buckskin jacket, faded canvas pants, and a red polka dotted bandanna that didn't look like one man would pick them all out.

Hofstede rode a tall, skinny blue roan horse that walked stiffly like it had been made to go very fast for a very long distance. At second glance, Garret reasoned the stiffness could merely mean the horse was getting old. There was a brand on his left hip that looked like a W with a line running through the middle third of it. It somehow looked fresh and old all at the same time, but before Garret could ask about it, he found himself meeting Hofstede's companions, Solomon, and George Lincoln.

Lincoln was built like a buffalo. He had the wild facial hair to accompany it too. He wasn't like the kind of buffalo that you would find on the Dakota plains during a cold winter when the scarce forage starved them. This man was like the buffalo you might see on a lucky hunting trip in a record rainfall year. He was massively built and hugely fat to boot. The draft horse he rode looked like it had seen more comfortable days pulling a whole cart instead of packing him around.

Solomon was a shorter, slender fellow. He had the dark complexion of a Prussian that would have been very pronounced if his companions hadn't had strong sun-tans. His beady brown eyes darted about with a subtle nervousness as he held his plain grey gelding's reins. He had said his last name but Garret didn't think he could even try to pronounce it. Besides, Garret quickly realized that the company only referred to him as Sol.

Garret ran inside to talk to Mrs. Heide while the visitors put their horses up. He could see Josh and the Boss off in the distance and wished they would hurry inside before the new men grew impatient. He was desperate to see the Boss hire on help for the cattle drive.

This opportunity seemed perfect; maybe even a little too perfect.

Loud chewing and boisterous laughter came from the dining room. Garret scooped another massive portion of mashed potatoes onto his plate and passed it on to Sol, who sat beside him. He'd gotten a positive first impression of the Prussian over the last couple hours. Despite the man's nervous nature, Garret was growing to like him. Most of the laughter came from the Boss. His deep, guttural chuckle went on and on as the listened to Hofstede tell well-rehearsed stories.

"So this city slicker hadn't ever had to milk a cow," Hofstede started. "The first time I tried to hand him the pail he told me he'd thought cowboys only rode horses and chased cows- like they do in the Wild West shows! He wasn't any good for that either! But anyway, where was I? Ah, yes. Well, I gave him an earful, and he went off to the barn.

127

This city boy came back without any milk, and I asked him what the matter was. He said he couldn't get the cow to hold still. So I hollered at him to tie her up and keep trying, and he went back to the barn. The second time he came back empty handed he said that the cow was too short. Having to crouch down by her udder cramped his legs. Now I was sure he was making excuses, but I gave him a stool and sent him off again.

He came back empty handed a third time! Can you believe that? I asked him what in the world the problem was now and he said to me, "It's not my fault! I can't get the cow to sit on the stool!"

The men were each a couple of glasses into the chokecherry wine, the only alcohol Mrs. Heide would allow at the supper table, and laughed hysterically. Dorothy rolled her eyes, but she was smiling.

"Oh John, tell them the story about your elk hunt," she suggested.

The company went on entertaining each other until there was hardly a scrap of food left to be found and Dorothy began clearing the table. When she sat out a strawberry-rhubarb pie, the room fell silent. Only little mm's of satisfaction assured the noisy bunch was still in the dining room at all.

The first to get through his share of the pie, the Boss pushed his chair back and fixed his gaze on the visitors.

"We can start the cattle drive early next week," he said. "There are still more cattle to sort out and brand. I expect it will take a full day to get everything packed."

"We?" Garret chimed in.

The Boss shot a scowl in Garret's direction. "By we, I mean you. I'm staying here with my ranch and my misses. Somebody's got to take care of them. Now, the trip down should take six or seven days if you don't run into any bad weather. You boys should know that the cattle have to be in Dillon by the end of the month, which isn't far away. You've got plenty of time to make it there without losing any heifers but no dilly-dallying."

"That would suit us just fine, sir," Hofstede said. "Do you have an idea of what you plan to pay for the job?"

John Heide glanced at Dorothy and then explained, "Thirty dollars a man for the drive to Dillon. Half of that is paid upfront. Josh will see to it that you get the rest when the cattle are on the train."

The offer sounded pretty good to Lincoln and Sol, who nodded their heads in agreement.

Hofstede's expression was unreadable. "Isn't the Dillon stockyard buying at a record high price?" he asked.

"It's a good price for replacement heifers," the Boss replied. "Last year there was a drought in the Midwest and a beef shortage back East because of it. Everyone butchered their cows to keep up with demand, and now they need more breeding stock."

"It's a good time to be in the cattle business then," Hofstede said.

"It makes up for some bad years." The Boss had a stern look covering his face. He knew what was coming next.

"I don't suppose you could do thirty-five dollars a hand for the boys and me," Hofstede said. "Share the good fortune with the market being so high."

The Boss's jaw was set hard. He wasn't pleased with Hofstede's suggestion, and he wasn't trying to hide it. He was already offering more than any other man in the county would pay to have cattle driven for seven days. Still, the extra few bucks didn't seem worth losing good help over.

"All right, I'll tell you what I'll do," he said. "If you boys make it to Dillon without losing any cattle; if every last one you started with gets loaded on that train, you'll each get a five dollar bonus."

Hofstede reached over the table, extending his hand. The two men shook hands firmly, sealing the deal.

The sunrise chased Josh and Garret out into the ranch yard. The days had been a blur of sorting cattle, loading saddlebags and tying down packs. Since there wasn't a cook wagon going on the drive, the boys loaded up two pack horses with all of their provisions. Slabs of bacon, packages of jerky, and other dry goods filled the saddlebags.

As always, Garret brought along a hand-me-down rifle, hoping to come by a rabbit or two. Though it would keep them alive on the trip, Josh wasn't looking forward to another round of Garret's cooking. The other men wouldn't have been either if they'd known just how bad a truly burnt biscuit could taste.

With the last pack tied down tightly, Josh led the men to the corrals, which nearly overflowed with sale heifers. The sea of red backs and white faces contrasted with the lush green grass sprouting on the ranch. The easy to spot cattle would make it even less excusable if the group were to lose a cow. Between the high price they would fetch at market and the pleasant lives they would lead in belly-high breadbasket pastures, Josh was determined to make it to Dillon with the full herd. The new hires, with less noble motives, were just as determined, even if it was only to put an extra dollar in the pocket.

Josh started on his black filly, who had earned the name Daisy. He was eager to show off the progress he'd made in training her. With Josh's encouragement, she followed the cows out of childlike curiosity. The timid heifers were still relatively small compared to most two-year-old mother cows and moved out of the horse's way quickly, giving Daisy confidence.

Leaving the ranch always felt like the beginning of something grand to Josh. He was a traveler by nature, though the opportunity seldom arose. He savored the unknown adventure found in open miles and the challenge of the inevitable minor disasters that occur on a cattle drive.

For Garret, the experience was quite the opposite. He was magnetically pulled towards the ranch. It was home. Leaving felt as unnatural and difficult as pulling a horseshoe nail off of a strong magnet – it could be done but the moment there was nothing left to pull it away, it would return instantaneously.

Mrs. Heide waved from the porch swing as her prized Hereford heifers left the ranch for the last time. It was hard to part with good animals – the result of years of backbreaking work and careful breeding- but the ranch couldn't afford to grow its operation, and

Dorothy knew that the heifers would serve a necessary purpose somewhere else.

The Boss had ridden out to doctor an injured calf just as the drive got underway. He hated to stand around and watch the cowboys leave without him, preferring to make himself busy elsewhere, so he felt useful.

Josh and Garret, who knew the way, rode at the front of the herd. Lincoln and Hofstede took the left and right flanks, darting off into the bushes to retrieve a runaway now and then. Sol took up the rear, riding drag, which he managed to do without complaining. Luckily for him, it was early enough in the year that the green grass kept the herd from kicking up much dust.

It was a leisurely morning. The cattle cooperated as best as cattle possibly can, seldom trying to turn back to the ranch. The drive took them across miles of neighboring ranch land. Occasionally, a rancher's kid would race out on horseback to wave at the passing sight.

One boy, probably ten or eleven by the looks of him, even gave his best speech to try to convince Josh to let him join the cattle drive. Taking him along was out of the question, but Josh liked the boy's gumption. He did his best to humor the kid.

"Sorry, son. We've got five men, and that's all we need," Josh said. "Next time we're looking for a new cowboy we'll come call on you."

The kid seemed satisfied enough with the answer. He turned and galloped his horse home as quickly as he could to brag to his brothers that he was in demand as a working cowboy.

It was around high noon before Sol abandoned his post at the back of the herd to find out if the group would have any dinner. His stomach had been grumbling for the last several miles. Between Josh's glaring response and Garret's laugh, Sol wasn't sure what the answer was. He continued glancing awkwardly between the two.

Josh didn't mind the man wanting something for a snack. What he didn't like was the risk of heifers turning around at the back of the herd while no one was there to urge them on. The foreman had an incredible ability to put food away, but to tell the truth he was also the sort of man who would forget about eating if his mind was set on work. He never quite realized that most other folks weren't the same way.

"I suppose you ought to take the other two some of these," he grumbled quietly, tossing Sol a bundle of leftover breakfast biscuits. Josh had spent all morning trying not to let the biscuits get smashed in his overstuffed pommel bags. They were stuck together with honey and jam that had leaked out of the sides, but the hungry cowboys wouldn't mind. They were already dusty and sweaty and being a little bit stickier wouldn't make much of a difference.

"Did you just give away all our food?" Garret asked after Sol had trotted off.

Without wasting any words, Josh took a smaller bundle out of his saddlebag and threw it to Garret, who mumbled his thanks between bites. Josh kept a handsome portion of the flaky biscuits for himself. He relished the taste, knowing it would be the last unburnt meal he'd be having for a while.

A full ten minutes probably hadn't passed before Garret spotted what he'd been keeping an eye out for all day. A fat cottontail rabbit sat in the shade of the nearby chokecherry bushes, unsuspecting. Faster than anyone could tell him not to, Garret slid off his horse, pushed the reins into Josh's hands, and crept away.

The rabbit still hadn't looked up from the patch of clover he was nibbling on. Garrett kneeled, steadying his shot. A loud bang rang out across the hills.

Even at the back of the herd, the heifers jumped. Sol's reaction scared them much worse than the gunshot alone had. He let out a strange scream and then hollered something to the effect of, "Don't shoot me!" in another language. His jump of fright had brought his legs tightly together and jabbed his spurs into his grey horse. The grey balked forward, lunging at the nearest cows who split in two directions and raced around the spooked horse. At that moment, Sol genuinely wished that he hadn't been left at the back of the herd alone.

Sol tried racing after the group of cows who had broken off from the herd, but he found that moving to get behind the strays only pushed them farther in the wrong direction. The Prussian sat dumbfounded. He felt angry that someone would shoot a gun so close to a cattle drive. No matter where he went, problems seemed to fall into Sol's lap.

As he sat brooding, the renegade cattle appeared to regain interest in following the rest of the herd. Sol let his horse stand very quietly while the Herefords meandered past him and then tried his best to catch them back up to the crowd. While Sol struggled to regain the scattered heifers at the rear of the herd, Josh and Garret argued over the rabbit.

"It's too hot out. That won't keep until suppertime," Josh said.

"It'll be fine," Garret argued.

"It's hot out here," Josh said again. "It'll be rotten by the time we make camp."

"Well, I know you're not going to let me stop long enough to clean it and cook it so what do you suggest I do with it?"

"Leave it for the coyotes. They'll be happy. You can find another one tonight. I don't know why you shot it in the first place."

"The coyotes can catch their own rabbit," Garret said, remounting. "This one's mine." With that, he loped off to the right-hand side of the herd, out of Josh's shouting range.

Following Josh's lead, the men funneled the cattle into an increasingly steep canyon. A wild river, bulging from snow runoff, accompanied them through the muddy red rock walls. Josh could only hope that none of the less intelligent cattle would try to wade in for a drink and be sucked into the river current. He glanced back periodically to see Lincoln and Hofstede in the distance, their expressions unreadable. Being so closed in made Josh uneasy.

Soon, the canyon gave out to into a vast valley. Josh could breathe a deep sigh of relief, having made it past the dangerous terrain. Here, the land was dotted with humble farmhouses and rimmed by proud mountains.

The cattle snatched up mouthfuls of wild grass as they continued across the miles.

It was nearly nightfall before any of the men spoke a word to one another. The long silent hours were good for the soul; or at least for Josh, who no longer cared much about Garret's rabbit hunt by the time they made camp. A moderate breeze had accompanied the crew through the Helena valley, offsetting the warmth of the sun. The wind had been a stroke of good luck for Garret. It kept his rabbit from spoiling before supper. He whistled an old tune while he cleaned and skinned the cottontail. He was cutting off a foot to save for good luck when Hofstede approached him.

"I suppose that's all for you," Hofstede said. He sat down next to Garret, his face friendly enough but his intent hard to read.

"I'll try to get another one here by that irrigation ditch," Garret replied, gesturing over his shoulder. "I've been here before. They like to hide in the tall grass." He felt awkward keeping the good stuff for only himself, but he had been the one doing the hunting. Still, Garret had been around the Heide's too long to not feed the company before he sank his teeth into a meal.

"Here, keep it," he said, pushing the rabbit at Hofstede. "See what you can do about cooking it up and I'll go after another one." With that, Garret snatched up his rifle and trudged off into the brush.

The camp was little more than a few flattened patches of grass that the men made by rolling out their bedrolls on the ground. A circle of stones serving as a campfire ring showed that it was a popular stopping point. Josh, Lincoln, and Hofstede arranged their sleeping places around the fire pit. Sol's consisted of nothing more than the Navajo blanket he had used for his saddle pad and a saddle bag for a pillow. Josh pitied him. It was going to be a cold night.

Hofstede got the fire going. He helped himself to Garret's cast iron skillet and a generous dose of salt to fry up some supper. He used his free hand to fiddle with his mustache and added sticks to the fire with the other. Before Hofstede had declared the meat cooked, Lincoln reached a large hand into the skillet and pulled out the biggest of the small chunks simmering over the fire.

"What do you think you're doing?" Hofstede hollered, swatting at Lincoln's hand.

The brawny man had already stuffed half of the piece in his mouth. It was still sweltering from being in the fire. He grunted, still trying to chew while the meat burned his tongue.

"Give me that," Hofstede hissed. His mustache twitched. He grabbed for the rabbit still halfway into Lincoln's mouth and tried to tear it out of the man's teeth. Josh sat by, unimpressed. It was the oddest game of tug-o-war he'd ever seen.

Sol's eyes went wide. In the commotion, he saw his chance to snatch up a piece of the scarce meat. A little wiser for Lincoln's mistake, he sat the prized scrap on his saddle bag to cool down. It was dark enough that no one would notice it was there.

"You boys know there's cornbread and beans in the packs, right?" Josh said, eyebrows raised.

It was a good thing for Josh that Garret returned at that moment to start frying beans. Josh was beginning to fear he might have anarchy on his hands if there wasn't more food available quickly. No other cottontails had crossed paths with Garret's rifle, but the cornbread and beans were a readily accepted substitute. The trio of new hires wasn't bothered much by the blackened edges on everything. It was apparent they didn't get very many decent meals in their travels.

The campfire crunched away at the firewood. The cowboys discovered how much cornbread each of their stomachs could hold, and the nearby cattle grazed lazily. As the temperature dipped, the stars came out. Thousands of them blanketed the world as Hofstede rode off to take the first shift watching over the cows. It was a cold but beautiful first night on the drive.

Chapter Seven

Garret's dark eyes scanned the cattle, counting. They were little more than vague blobs of color on the dark landscape. He wasn't sure at what point the herd ended, and the hay fields began. The cowboy had taken the last shift of night-watch to make sure no stray dogs or other pests bothered the herd. The night had been quiet and peaceful.

Most of the cattle had bedded down next to the irrigation ditch with no desire to leave. A few heifers wandered across the grass, stretching their tired legs and grabbing an occasional nighttime snack. Garret's colt, Pocket, dozed along with the cows, while Garret watched the disappearing constellations. The young ranch hand knew how to find the big soup ladle and the little soup ladle, but the rest of the stars were a mystery to him.

An owl called out and fell silent. Garret glanced behind himself at a grove of scraggly trees. The night hunter perched on a low branch, yellow eyes glowing in the dark. Garret watched the bird silently while a streak of grey light in the sky grew gradually wider, replacing blackness.

It was so early in the morning that most of the earth still considered it nighttime. Even the early-rising birds hadn't started singing yet. The campfire had all but burned out during the night. Josh used the dying embers to light a new bundle of kindling and started scrounging around for coffee grounds. The coffee was one thing he would never leave up to Garrett.

The foreman sat with his boots inside the fire ring, stretching his hands forward to warm them over the faint blaze. The cowboys still in the camp, which consisted of the new hires, hadn't stirred. Josh felt he might as well be there all alone. Josh liked being alone in the mornings. It gave him a moment to recharge and pray for the coming day. With the crew he'd acquired, it was going to take a lot of praying to get to Dillon.

He didn't own a Bible aside from the one Mrs. Heide had lent him, which was in German. Josh didn't read German, but he did know the gist of the gospel. The foreman even had a few verses memorized, in English of course. He hoped to buy a new Bible at the end of the drive or on the return trip. It just seemed hard to happen upon one at a time that he had money in his pocket.

Though Josh was a frugal man, he was generous to a fault. He'd gladly give his wages away when he went to church once a month, reasoning that he didn't need the money for anything important. He certainly wasn't saving up for a ranch. In fact, the foreman wasn't concerned if he ever left the Heide operation. Having a place all his own might feel too lonely.

The sound of galloping hooves broke the silence. Josh looked up, startled to find Garret charging his horse straight for the campfire. Pocket screeched to a halt barely an inch from the fire pit, his front shoes almost grazing the rocks. He tossed his head defiantly.

"Two cows missing," Garret huffed. He had a wild look in his eyes that seemed to say he was exaggerating the situation.

Josh slowly rose to his feet. "Did you look through the trees?" he asked, trying to calm Garret down. He grabbed Pocket's bridle with one hand and pushed the colt back away from the fire. Garret's urgency hadn't sunk in yet.

"Yeah I checked there," Garret said, still breathing heavily. "Checked the trees. Checked the ditch. Checked a quarter mile in every direction."

Kicking the campfire coal off the soles of his boots, Josh arched his back, trying to stretch out the stiffness of the cold morning. When he didn't say anything, Garret spoke again.

"Hello?" He prodded. "We are missing cows. Our bonus, which was all my bacon for the winter, went and wandered off. Now, are you going to help find them or are you going to stretch?"

"Count them again," Josh replied.

"No. they're gone."

"They're probably there. I know I sometimes miscount too."

"You might miscount, but I don't, and I especially don't miscount three times."

Garret impatiently waited while Josh rubbed a calloused hand over the back of his neck. The cowboy finally turned and rode away before another word was exchanged. He was gone for the rest of the hour. Josh packed up his bedroll and sat eating whatever wasn't squished in his pommel bags while the other men dozed.

When the light was stronger, he went down to the ditch and carried back a bucketful of water that he boiled. The ranch-worker didn't trust the cleanliness of water that came from a highly populated valley, especially not from an open ditch. A tenth of the water he put in his canteen and the rest he saved for the others.

Finally, Garret reappeared. He rode towards camp at a fast trot but stopped well before the fire this time. The hair that hung over his forehead was tinted with sweat. He sat a moment, catching his breath before he gave his report.

"We are missing two," he said. "To make it worse, they're my two."

The Boss had allowed Garret to keep a small number of his cows on the ranch for several years. He never had more than ten, which didn't do much damage on a spread that occupied hundreds of cows. Every couple of years, Garret culled a handful of the bovines from his herd to sell. It could be nothing but the worst of bad luck that the only two heifers

Garret had brought along to market this year happened to be the ones that went missing.

"I rode as far west as I could until I ran into a ranch and it's all fenced off," Garret continued. "I talked to one of their cowboys. He hasn't seen any Herefords roaming around, but they'll corral them if they wander along. Last night was silent. I still don't know what could have scared two cows off, unless they were already gone before I started watching the herd." Garret's face hinted that he meant something by his last statement.

He was a better night watchman than anyone Josh had ever known. If heifers disappeared on Garret's watch, they might as well be ghosts. If the missing cows had been gone since before Garret took over in the middle of the night, they had quite a head start. That was what worried Josh.

"Why didn't you come to get me sooner?" Josh asked, dumbfounded. He stared at Garret, his mind slowly starting to register the reality that they had already lost two cows.

"You weren't much help the last time I asked," Garret replied sarcastically.

Josh glanced around the camp. Hofstede was casually watching the conversation unfold. Sol had woken up but sat sheepishly on his Navajo blanket, staring at rocks on the ground. Only Lincoln still slumbered and would probably continue to until someone nudged a boot into his side hard enough to wake him up. He finally looked back to Garret's worried eyes and nodded. "Let's go find them."

Garret turned to the new hires with the shadow of blame on his face. "You three stay here!" he barked. "And don't lose any more!" As if his words demanded action, he trotted off to the loose horses and threw a rope around Old Bay for Josh to saddle.

The foreman wasn't thrilled to have the chain of command broken, but considering the situation, he figured there were more important things to worry about than who was saying orders that needed to be said. Josh lifted his saddle, propping it on his hip and glanced behind himself. "Get him up for crying out loud!" he yelled, looking at Lincoln.

Having given his final decree, Josh saddled and bridled Old Bay as quickly as he could. The pair of riders took off. Skirting east of the herd, they continued along the ditch bank. There was nothing in this direction except for flat hay ground, and before long the irrigation ditch made a ninety-degree turn, blocking them off from the fields beyond. Quick water rushed down the steep, wide ditch.

As they approached the corner, the riders nearly walked over a small whitetail buck who had been hiding in the tall grass. The wild animal leaped up, white tail raised in alarm. His two-point antlers glistened with dew in the morning shade. The deer cleared the ditch in one natural bound and raced across the hay fields until he was no bigger than a dime on the horizon.

Without a word, Garret turned Pocket around on his haunches and long-trotted back the direction he had come. Guessing the ranch hand would eventually turn south, Josh headed that way, sticking near to the ditch bank. He was partially glad to be away from his brooding company. Losing valuable cattle was no small problem but at the same time, hoarding a chest-full of anger at the world's great jokes wouldn't help find missing cows.

Taking a slow breath, Josh tried to think where he would have gone if he had been a lost cow. It wasn't very likely that a cow would have attempted the jump over the ditch. They lacked the gracefulness and athleticism of a deer. Cows took the path of least resistance instead. One patch of grass led them to another, and they typically meandered in totally illogical zig-zags.

He theorized that cows wandered and ate grass selectively for the health of the range. God had probably decided that if a beast who weighed well over thirteen-hundred pounds ate every blade she came across, it wouldn't be long before there was no grass left in the world. A few blades left behind could go to seed and make more grass for the following year. Now wasn't the time for theories though. It was time for searching. With no more idea of what might go on inside a missing cow's brain, Josh urged Old Bay onward.

The morning took Josh down one hay field after another. Purple flowers graced the tips of the growing alfalfa. A few farmers were out in the fields putting up their first cutting of hay for the summer. Josh approached an elderly man who drove a swather pulled by heavy Percheron horses. The man's two grown sons worked at mending a nearby beaver-slide, a tall wooden contraption that allowed loose hay to be catapulted into huge stacks. The family was friendly but the only thing they'd seen all morning was hay.

Josh could only hope that Garret had already found the two heifers and brought them back to camp. He figured Hofstede must have taken the first watch at about nine o'clock the previous night. With the noon sun hanging high above him, the cows could be fifteen hours from camp by now.

Of course, cows wouldn't move very far in an hour unless horses and cowboys were pushing them. With this in mind, Josh decided to cut west. There were still a few shelter-belts of thick, scraggly trees and bushes on the horizon. With the heat of the sun glaring down, they would have made a nice place for a cow to stop and rest in the shade.

Old Bay tried to turn back towards camp several times. His dark muzzle drifted that direction, and his eye stayed focused to the south even while he silently obeyed the order to walk on. The old horse seemed to have accepted the truth before anyone else could. Josh had no hope of finding the missing cows.

As the hours ticked by, Josh's initial panic faded into numbness. He had found every deer, cottontail, and wandering barn cat in that part of the valley. From the lack of tracks or other evidence, it had been months since any cows had crossed that stretch of country at all. Josh was near to the path the drive had taken when he spotted Garret's horse ambling in slow motion. He was rider-less.

From here, Josh could see that the sorrel colt was limping, but he couldn't tell which foot was sore. Old Bay broke into a lope almost the instant Josh thought of it. Pocket picked his head up, whinnying at his approaching fried. Josh readied himself to catch the loose horse. He didn't want to have to think about finding the rider yet.

Just as Josh got in range to snatch up Pocket's reins, he realized that a set of human legs was barely visible on the far side of the horse. Garret was there after all. He held his tan straw hat, using it as a fan. The dark-haired cowboy walked alongside his limping colt, his gait a little stiff. Pocked hadn't stopped sweating since that morning and Garret didn't look much better. His desperate eyes searched Josh, saying he hadn't seen any sign of the heifers either.

"I want to look just a little ways further," Garret said.

"What happened to Pocket?" Josh asked.

"I think he must have stepped on a sharp rock."

"Can you tell which foot?" Josh stepped down off of Old Bay to get a closer look. The two men looked over Pocket's hooves, but nothing was obviously wrong with any of them.

Eventually, Garret repeated himself. "I'd been wanting to go just a little further back towards the canyon to check for those heifers."

With another look at Pocket, Josh knew that Garret wasn't going to make it that far on foot. "Here, take Old Bay," he offered. The men traded horses and Josh began the long walk back to camp, leading the limping colt.

When he returned, Sol was attempting to watch the herd, which he wasn't doing very well. His nervousness shot through his horse and the grey gelding pranced about, spooking the heifers. Josh took his time untacking Pocket and gave him a good rub down. He turned the colt loose and watched him limp to the other horses. Only then did the foreman start to worry about what the rest of the crew was doing. He found them sitting on their saddle blankets next to the fire pit.

Hofstede had talked Lincoln into a game of cards. The large man had nothing to bet except for a stash of whiskey that he would have rather died than give up, so he put up a dollar of his unearned wages. Lincoln looked overconfident, like he didn't understand that he was going to lose. Even if Hofstede hadn't been cheating, Lincoln wouldn't have stood a chance against him. Luckily for him, Josh kneeled and scooped up the playing cards before the game could be decided.

"There are rules around here," Josh said, his irritation overcoming his shyness. He paused, fidgeting with his sunken hat brim before he went on. "No gambling. No drinking. No chasing after girls. What you do with your time when the drive is over is your own business. Until then, we've got a job to do, and we're doing it pretty poor so far." He tucked the cards into his shirt pocket and walked away.

It was the middle of the night when Garret returned to camp. Josh had sent the other cowboys out looking for him while he kept the herd where they were. Garret rode in without the lost cows. He had been awake for over twenty-four hours. Even considering all of that, he looked almost happy.

"Those cows never made it past the canyon," Garret swore. "Fred Miller found them lost in the woods like a couple of pieces of bear bait."

Garret pulled a coin pouch out of his coat pocket and rattled it.

"I sold them to Miller," Garret announced. His eyes were completely bloodshot from lack of sleep. "I figure if this crew can't drive them one full day without them getting lost, I should get some money for them while I can." He sat down for, "just a minute," and fell fast asleep before that minute was up.

The next morning, the drive carried on. Boulders leaned against the sky, propped up by the foothills. Great mountains crept up to the backs of the boulders in the east and west. The path grew narrow once more. Garret all but slept in his saddle, floating along with the sea of bovines. He was glad to feel like the worst challenge was behind him.

Chapter Eight

Fragrant pink petals overwhelmed Kaitlyn's senses. She flushed the same bright color as the store bought flowers J.B. Wylie had just handed her. Since their dinner together, he had stopped at the schoolhouse with increasing frequency. At first, she had tried to time her after school rides to avoid his visits. He was quick to catch on to her routine but not to the message that she wasn't interested in his company.

"Thank you," Kaitlyn stammered.

Wylie watched her reaction closely. He seemed a little nervous himself. "I thought we could ride together today since you're so fond of a ride in the afternoon," he said.

Kaitlyn looked around behind her, hoping for an excuse to present itself. "Oh, I have so much work to grade," she said. There wasn't a single paper on her desk but it was the best reason she could invent. "I don't think I have time to go riding today."

"You're already dressed for it," Wylie replied.

The schoolteacher looked down at her brown riding skirt. She had thrown it on the moment school had ended, hoping to be a mile out of town before Mr. Wylie stopped in to see her. She hadn't been quick enough. Now her appearance betrayed her.

"Well, yes, I did dress to ride, but I've been feeling pretty tired today," Kaitlyn babbled. "I might change my mind about going."

"Perhaps a stroll through town instead," Wylie said, offering his arm.

Making the excuse that she needed to put the flowers in some water, Kaitlyn retreated back into the schoolhouse. Wylie followed her eagerly. He sat down, dwarfing his desk of choice. Kaitlyn couldn't help but laugh at the sight, which her new suitor took as a victory. While he seemed to be gaining ground, Wylie continued.

"We could walk past the stores on Main Street before closing. I know there's a new shipment in at the saddlery and you might see something you like."

Kaitlyn shook her head. The last thing she wanted to accept was an expensive gift from Wylie. Even if he did have the money to throw away, she didn't want the implications that came with taking it. "A ride would be fine," she said.

Wylie's ranch started at the opposite edge of town, near the railroad tracks. From there, it stretched back miles into the high desert foothills. The land was nothing too beautiful, but there certainly was a lot of it. Stalks of grass, exhausted from the wind, bobbed between faded sagebrush, competing for space on the rangeland. Rows and rows of cross fencing divided the scenery. A colonial style house sat on the highest ridge overlooking the property.

The riders averted the ridge where the main house stood. Instead, they passed underneath a towering wooden archway onto a road that dissected the vast spread. The two rode past a seemingly endless stockyard filled with cattle from different ranches.

"These will all ship out on the next train," Wylie mentioned.

For once, Wylie was relatively quiet. It was hard to tell whether he'd grown tired of bragging about himself or if he thought his property could do the bragging for him. Either way, Kaitlyn was content to ride in the comfortable silence. The wind hadn't come up that evening, and its absence felt luxurious.

It was a surprisingly long ride to cover even just a section of the operation. Wylie fidgeted with his mustache or straightened his saddle more often than he spoke. The black gelding he rode knew the route without any aid from a rider. When they reached another wooden archway, the gelding turned around automatically to retrace his route home.

The fading evening made Wylie's ranch look like an oil painting. It was all delicate brush strokes and carefully blended paint. Intricately detailed horses frozen in still motion. Towering barns splashed up against a sunset sky.

"This is the place I always dreamed of having," Wylie said proudly. Kaitlyn glanced sideways at him. His eyes softened, taking in the scene with wonder as if he'd never seen it before. His innocent expression made Kaitlyn think there had once been a kind boy beneath all the hard years. "Does it remind you of home?" he asked. Kaitlyn bit her lip, staring out into the fields.

"No," she finally replied. "But it is beautiful in its own way."

As they rode back to the schoolhouse, Kaitlyn caught sight of Lacey frantically waving to her. Knitting yarn covered the front porch where she stood. Strings tangled around her feet and every time she tried to free herself from the mess, another strand ensnared her.

"I'd better go talk to her," Kaitlyn said. "Have a good night," she added over her shoulder. For once, Mr. Wylie was content to end the conversation and ride away. Kaitlyn tied Dolly up quickly and followed Lacey's beckoning waves.

"What happened?" Kaitlyn asked, looking around at the yarn.

"Oh, never mind that. I couldn't find the color I wanted," Lacey replied.

Kaitlyn crouched down to begin picking up the loose yarn.

"Are you getting engaged?" Lacey asked. Her voice wasn't concealing any excitement, and she drew each of the vowels out for too long.

"No!" Kaitlyn protested. "I do not like him."

"Well, he certainly likes you!" Lacey gushed. "Oh, and when you marry him, you'll be the richest woman in town! Maybe in the whole state! We can have tea at your mansion and throw balls and banquets!"

"Great. I'll start writing the guest list of all of the people I want to have over for a tea party," Kaitlyn said dryly. Aside from Lacey, she rarely spoke to anyone in town.

Sarcasm was usually lost on Lacey. "Oh my! Your wedding is going to be just huge!" she continued.

"Lacey," Kaitlyn tried to cut in.

"I can just imagine your dress! Long train, lots of lace, pure white. It's going to be perfect! It will swish around when you dance! Oh, I do hope you'll have dancing at the wedding."

"Lacey, stop!"

Lacey paused with more words hanging halfway out of her mouth.

Kaitlyn placed her hands firmly on Lacey's shoulders and looked her dead in the eyes. "I. Am. Not. Getting. Married." She gave Lacey a good shake before letting go.

"But, but," Lacey pleaded.

"No!" Kaitlyn turned to leave. Lacey tried to follow but found herself too tangled up to go anywhere. Kaitlyn was free to storm down the short stretch of street to the schoolhouse.

Wedged in the door-frame was a dirty envelope. It looked like it had been dropped in the mud and then dried. Ducking inside, Kaitlyn tore it open and read the first page.

Our Dear Kaitlyn,

We're doing well here on the ranch, thank you for asking. The calves have been strong and healthy this year. Your Grandpa decided to keep the palomino filly you liked so much. He's calling her Blondie. My health has returned. I feel like I'm young again. We still miss seeing you and Dolly riding in the pastures. The boys will see you soon when they bring the sale cows down to Dillon. I hope you are well. You always had such a love for teaching. Grandpa and I are proud to see you following that dream. Write to us soon, please.

Isaiah 40:31 'But those who wait on the Lord shall renew their strength; they shall mount up on wings like eagles, they shall run and not be weary, they shall walk and not faint.'

Love Grandma and Grandpa Heide

The second page had two sets of writing on it – one from Josh and one from Garret.

Dear Teacher,

How are the students treating you? The ranch is quiet without you. Josh's grammar has gotten terrible. He keeps saying things like "wasn't none" and I can't get him to fix it. We can't figure out how to count the cows either without someone who's

good at math. You'll just have to come back home and get it straightened out.
Your friend, Garret James

Kaitlyn reread what Garret had written. He'd always been such a jokester. His handwriting was thin, flowing, and perfect. In contrast, Josh's was barely legible.

Hi Kaitlyn. I'm glad you wrote. The Boss was getting worried. We'll be in Dillon at the end of the month. How is school?
Joshua Challis

Gently replicating the folds, Kaitlyn tucked the letters under her arm. She imagined how the words would sound coming from their writers' mouths. Her blue eyes pictured their faces, their expressions. She could almost see Garret's sarcastic smile as he called her teacher. She placed the letters side by side on her bed to read again later.

Chapter Nine

The cattle drive reached the valley's end by midday. Garret rode drag, claiming the excuse that he didn't want to wear out a second horse. Missy Lew was far too much of a pretty show-pony type to ride the dusty drag position. A mane full of trail dirt didn't become her, and she made her complaints known, tossing her head and jittering left and right. Garret kept her lined out until she accepted her dusty fate and resigned to a more reasonable pace.

Every once in a while, a horse came out of ranch-bred lines that would rather plod through town carrying an elegant rider than work cattle. There was a good market for these pleasure horses if they were smooth, well built, and beautiful. Between her shimmering buckskin coat and her easy gaits, Missy Lew fit the bill. Garret did not doubt that a rancher's wife or daughter or even a refined gentleman would offer a high price to make the filly a pleasure mount at the trail's end. For now, she would have to work like everyone else if they were going to make it to Dillon on time.

As it was, the crew was already going to have to hurry just to fit in their mandatory detour to the trapper's cabin. Any long business trip, including the cattle drive, usually meant running other odd errands for the Boss along the way.

Today's miscellaneous task was delivering payment to Waylon, the fur trapper who kept the ranch a little safer from invasive wolves. Josh had never met the man before, but he was familiar with the stereotype that trappers tended to be unsociable.

Josh was at least halfway sure he knew how to find the trapper's place. He took Solomon and Lincoln with him, leaving Garret and Hofstede to hold the herd. Josh glanced ahead wearily as they followed a narrow gulch that cut through the side of the hills. He hadn't personally known anyone to have a horse's leg get caught in a trap, but he'd heard stories. The idea made him shudder. Luckily, Josh didn't have much time to dwell on the thought before the mountains opened up into a homestead.

Thick aspen trees huddled around an odd collection of log sheds and lean-tos. There wasn't a soul in sight. Josh dismounted and handed his reins to Solomon.

"I'll see if he's home," Josh said. He knew the trapper wasn't used to having much company and could be a bit jumpy if someone wandered in unannounced. The last thing anyone wanted was for old Waylon to mistake the party of cowboys for an ambush and start shooting. Josh figured his chances of avoiding a shot made by a professional hunter were pretty slim.

"You two wait here," Josh ordered, looking behind himself at Sol and Lincoln. Josh wandered forward, hoping there weren't any traps hidden in the clearing. Under the closest lean-to, a red fox pelt hung beside a badger who still looked like he might bite, with or without breath in his lungs. The hair on the back of Josh's neck tensed just looking at the snarling teeth. He was glad he hadn't encountered the badger when it was still alive.

Josh looked back apprehensively to where he had left his companions. They were gone. Already. He wondered how he had lost track of them so quickly. The foreman had begun to hate the feeling that he had to babysit half of his crew. Josh shook his head. There was no point in looking for Sol and Lincoln. They would turn up eventually. Instead, he went on looking for signs of the trapper.

Making new outbuildings seemed to be the trapper's second hobby. Rough cut poles made up storage spaces for elk hides, neatly organized steel traps, and odd furs. One squatty shed even had a small milk cow tied inside. None of the buildings Josh came across looked quite like a cabin though.

Finally, Josh peered around the corner of the last shed standing in the crooked row. There wasn't much space between the backs of the shack and the hillside. The tiny area that was there appeared to be empty aside from a dog sled that sat waiting for winter. There didn't seem to be anywhere else to look for the house. The trapper might have been living amidst the outbuildings after all.

A deafening crack rang out through the clearing. Josh turned around quickly to see Lincoln standing beneath a shed, his face contorted in pain. Waylon stood holding an ax, the blunt end of which he'd used to smack Lincoln's hand away from an elk hide.

"Quit touching that!" he spat. "I don't want grubby fingers all over it."

Waylon had appeared silently but didn't seem surprised that the group was there. Josh knew instantly, without having to be told, that the person he was looking at was Waylon. The man was built like an oak tree or a mountain-depending on what kind of a mountain was nearby. A plateau would have been a pretty close comparison. If he'd eaten a few more meals in a day, Waylon could have overtaken Lincoln as the largest man Josh had ever seen.

The towering figure was clad in finely stitched buckskin and fur that made Josh wonder if his old cowboy clothes looked like rags. He had long, plain brown hair that matched his beard and brown eyes nearly the same color. With a little green paint, he could have very easily camouflaged into the landscape.

"Boss!" Lincoln howled, for help.

Josh, who wasn't used to being called the boss of the operation, didn't respond. The trapper turned his attention to Josh who quickly stepped forward to announce their business before anyone else came to blows with the trapper's ax-handle, or worse.

"I'd be glad if you could get him to keep his hands to himself," Waylon grunted. His voice was deep and booming. Listening to him was like standing next to a cannon. It almost hurt Josh's ears.

"Sir," Josh stammered. "John Heide asked me to deliver your pay." He emphasized the Boss's name, hoping it would somehow get him out of trouble.

A change came over the trapper's eyes. "Sure! You're the foreman, aren't you?" The burly man sat his ax down against a shed wall. Josh shook his outstretched hand, which was covered in fading scars and newer scabs. "You bring my money?" Waylon asked.

Eager to be on the trapper's good side, Josh hurriedly handed over his delivery of gold pieces. Waylon examined them. He turned the shining metal over in his hands. Excitement brightened his plain brown features. He was nothing more than a giant kid. A giant kid who killed the West's most dangerous animals.

Suddenly, Waylon seemed to remember something. "My wife's got that coat ready," he said. Without explaining anything, he gestured for Josh to follow. Afraid to refuse, Lincoln came along reluctantly.

The trapper ducked behind the sheds and strode towards the steepest part of the hillside. Now that he was looking at it, Josh wondered how he hadn't seen the door before. It sat level to the land, leading into the dirt like a mine shaft. A chimney poked out of the hill above. Josh was surprised that no dirt fell away when Waylon opened the door.

"Come on in," he said over his shoulder. The trapper's air had become casual and friendly despite the fact he had clobbered one of his visitors just a few minutes ago.

Though he wasn't sure how he'd gotten there, Josh found himself and his whole crew of cowboys seated around an oak table. He had accepted Waylon's offer to let the group stay for the night and use a roughly fenced pasture out back for the cattle. The field was only inhabited by one horse who was too old to ride and a mammoth mule. When the mule wouldn't make due, the trapper used his dog sled team to commute.

Josh hadn't seen any of the sled dogs earlier because the massive huskies inhabited an entryway into the underground house. The long, narrow room appeared to be another stack of furs until it became evident that their chests were rising and falling. It was pleasantly cool inside the hillside, despite the dozen large dogs. The Huskies slept placidly, waiting for the evening when it wouldn't be so hot outside.

The house itself was built deep into the side of the hill. Hundreds of stones cemented together made up the inside walls and kept the hillside from coming into the rooms. Kerosene lanterns placed about the room made up for the lack of natural sunlight. The floor was a series of handmade bricks, partially covered with woven rugs. The fireplace sat dormant in the corner with a bearskin spread out beneath it.

The trapper's wife, a charming Indian girl, was setting food on the table. Waylon had introduced her as Mary Ruth. The native woman's hair was held back by a sterling silver comb. Her earrings were dangling turquoise beads. She might have been mistaken for the daughter of a chief for the wealth shown in her jewelry. Most noticeably, Mary Ruth had a handsome but stern expression that made the cowboys think they'd better mind their table manners for once.

Four small girls bounced around the room. All barefoot, they leaped from rug to rug in a game the adults could not have understood. They took turns carrying the littlest, a boy who was lucky not to have been dropped by any of his rambunctious sisters.

Whenever he was set down for a moment, he made his most desperate attempt to crawl to the stack of fur blankets in the corner of the room. A child his size could have hidden there. To his disgruntlement, he never made it to safety before another sister scooped him up and carried him off.

For once, the rowdy new hires were quiet. Garret and Waylon had been carrying on a conversation about wildlife management that they both seemed to find very important.

"The problem starts when all these people who don't know a timber wolf from a house cat try to get involved," Waylon said.

Both Garret and Waylon had taken part in virtually the same conversation many times. They both enjoyed reciting it over again every time they found someone who shared their view.

"I'd like to see them cry to save the wolves when the savages carry off their favorite pet," Garret replied.

"Exactly!" Waylon agreed. "Some folks just don't think it through."

"When it's not their backyard, they always want anything and everything to run wild and free and have it all left alone," Garret said, rolling his eyes.

"Neglect is not conservation, my boy," Waylon interjected. "Do you think we would have any mule deer left in ten years if someone didn't control the population of predators? Those Canadian beasts terrorizing your ranch are meant to be up chasing after caribou."

Garret nodded his approval.

Waylon carried on, "I don't do any hunting without reason. Wolves kill because they enjoy killing. I can't tell you how many wolf-killed deer carcasses I found that weren't even half eaten. Man's dominion over the earth is a sacred duty. It's his job to bring things back into balance when they start getting out of hand. That's why a good woodsman hunts what needs to be hunted and lets the rest go so they can repopulate."

Mary Ruth sat at the table, placing herself in the middle of their conversation. "Yes, but if I weren't here, you boys would have nothing to do but hunt the whole forest down. It's not good that a man should be alone," she said with a laugh.

Waylon seemed to be finished with his speech anyway. He passed a basket of cornbread to Garret, and they moved on to different subjects. Josh chimed in when he could but mostly found himself nodding along. More than once, he had to force his eyes away from staring at the comb in Mary Ruth's hair. She spoke here and there, and when she did, everyone listened.

The new hires were too quiet, Solomon especially. He gave only one or two-word answers, mostly elicited by Mary Ruth. Both Hofstede and Lincoln seemed deliberately tight-lipped. They sat unusually straight in their chairs, muscles tensed, with their eyes on their food.

When the meal had been cleared, Waylon's towering figure rose from his chair. He spanned the room in two strides and collected a thick red coat from the corner. He traced a burly hand over the coat's stitching before handing it to Josh. "I had Ruth put on some extras. Sure hope Mrs. Heide don't mind. I hate to have good material sitting around going to waste."

"I'm sure she'll like it," Josh offered. The coat was made of carefully stitched fox fur. He let his raw fingers sink into the plush red pelt. The extras Waylon had been referring to were tassels that decorated the back. Josh didn't bother to wonder how much the coat was worth, but he knew Mrs. Heide would look more elegant than the high society ladies on the East Coast.

"I never used to get foxes out here," Waylon said, "Now there've been too many foxes. Hardly any rabbits left because of them. Ruth makes a good rabbit stew, and I've got to have rabbits around for that, so I cut the fox population back."

Josh nodded, not quite as rehearsed in the repeating wildlife management conversation as Garret. "It's sure nice," he finally said. Without meaning to, he had addressed the comment to Mary Ruth. Her dark brown eyes smiled. She took the coat out of Josh's hands.

"I'll wrap it up," she said.

Although there was no need to watch the livestock that night, Josh lay awake, propped up by the pasture fence. The other cowboys slept beneath one shed or another. Unable to sleep, Josh had done some walking to clear his head. His walk had led him to the crooked fence where he stared between the night sky and the grazing cattle.

His mind was stuck on the trapper's wife. What she had said resounded like an echo. "It's not good that man should be alone." Cowboys survived doing plenty of things that weren't good for them. Josh had broken both of his legs at one point or another. He regularly worked a full day on three or four hours of sleep. None of that bothered him. It was the lonely years, one after another, that he was starting to notice.

In the bleak state of Montana, it was no easy task to come by a lady friend. The ones who weren't married were awful, and the ones that were only a little bit awful were already engaged. Settling down was hard and getting by alone was getting harder.

The foreman didn't think much of it, but he was aware the girls in town found him handsome. Again, the ones who weren't taken weren't much good. Dance hall girls repulsed him. He knew he ought to just feel sorry for the women who had no home and no other way to survive, but he couldn't muster up much pity. He wasn't going to share a girl's attention. Especially not with everyone in town.

Thinking back, Josh recalled that one of his old friends had married a dance hall girl. She'd been plain and plump. The woman must not have owned a clear mirror judging by her opinion of herself. She thought that she was the most desired woman on the earth and she convinced her husband of it. He was constantly tortured by jealousy. She'd made him into a fool. In Josh's opinion, that was worse than being alone.

No wiser on the subject of women, he decided it was time to return to his bedroll amidst the sheds. If he couldn't sleep, he could at least spend some time resting with his eyes closed. The foreman rose and dusted off his pant legs. Twigs crunched under his feet as he walked.

There was another sound in the night. Before Josh had even seen the new hire, he felt Solomon's elbows knock into him. The scrawny man's arms were wrapped around a ball of red and grey that took on new shapes in the moonlight. As Sol squeezed the bundle tighter, it became more oblong until part of it escaped his grasp and fell to the ground.

Josh bent forward to scoop up the fallen object. Only when his fingers made contact did he realize what it was. Solomon's arms were full of stolen furs. The foreman glanced to the nearest lean-to, where half a dozen fox furs had been tanning. The shed now stood vacant.

Shock came over Josh's features. "I assume this wasn't a gift from Ruth and Waylon," he said dryly.

Solomon stared back. At least his eyes were focused for once. His jaw jutted out at a crooked angle while he chewed on the inside of his cheek.

Josh rocked back on his heels, staring at the sky. There had never been a thief on his crew. Suddenly Solomon's darting eyes made sense.

"You didn't pay for those," Josh spat, pointing at the furs. He waited for Solomon to speak up for himself. To apologize, argue, draw a gun, anything. Still, the man stood silent.

"I'd better see those all hanging back where they came from by morning or you're getting hung!" Josh felt trigger-shy as soon as the words left his tongue. A hot rage lit his gut, but his hands felt unbearably cold.

Suddenly, the dam inside Solomon broke. He ranted violently in a language Josh couldn't understand. His tone showed not an ounce of remorse. Somewhere, the words, "fair," and, "slave," and, "home," broke from the pack of slurred English. Finally, he sank to the ground, sobs pouring from his eyes. His shoulders heaved. He released the mass of furs onto the dusty earth and stared at them.

A hard feeling had spread over Josh's chest. He couldn't feel sorry for the man - not yet. Whatever Sol was showing, it wasn't repentance. "Listen," Josh said, pulling him up by the collar. "We've all had hard knocks in life. You're not a prince in a golden castle? Tough. I don't owe you anything, but I'm giving you one chance to get it straight! If you don't take your chance, I'm sure Waylon's got a strong tree. Now, you'd better put Waylon's things back where you got them!"

He dropped his hold on the Prussian's neck. Sol's collar stretched, he sunk the six inches back to the ground. Though Josh trembled, Solomon now stood stock still. There was nothing else to say. Josh turned to go. As an afterthought, he wheeled around and dealt the bandit a solid punch in the nose. Sol groaned loudly, covering his face, while the foreman walked away.

Throughout the night, Josh fought the urge to alert Garret or Waylon. He comforted himself with the thought that even if Solomon took off in the night, he wouldn't be able to make it out through the steep gulch before morning. It would be no contest if he and Garret needed to catch up to a thief. Josh hoped he wouldn't have to take chase though. Solomon didn't deserve a chance. There was little doubt that he'd blown his chance before. Still, Josh found himself giving the nervous scoundrel a shot.

When the grey light met with the dawn, Josh rose to gather his horses. He took the long route to the pasture, making his way past the place he had found Solomon the night before. Josh's breath was deliberate until he saw a row of fox-pelts draped up as if they had never left at all. He sighed and walked on quickly. Even being near the expensive pelts made him uncomfortable considering the previous night's events. It had never been Josh's neck on the line, but he felt relief like it had been.

With his fingers still shaking intermittently, the foreman saddled Old Bay and loaded his bedroll on Pepper. The speckled filly hadn't seen many riding miles so far on the trail. Josh had been using the excuse he needed to keep her fresh if he was going to sell her in Dillon. He promised himself he would switch to using Pepper tomorrow. He knew his nerves might set the young horse off if he tried to leg her up today.

While Josh was tightening his pack strings, he caught sight of Garret and Waylon walking the pasture. He watched from a distance as Garret led Pocket back to the trapper. The colt still limped noticeably. Waylon picked up each hoof in turn and tapped on it with a piece of metal, testing for soreness. When he got to the right front foot, Pocket flinched sharply. His ears shot back against his head.

Waylon didn't release his hoof right away, and the sorrel bent around to nip at him. Garret had grown used to the colt's antics. He was quick enough to intervene before Pocket made a snack of the trapper's ear. Waylon dropped the colt's foot and turned to start what looked like a serious conversation with Garret.

Josh couldn't know if Waylon was onto Solomon's coveting issue. It occurred to him for the first time that if his crew rode off with Waylon's belongings, the burly mountaineer might not be picky about who got hung for the trespass. Rather than say too much, Josh turned his attention to moving the cows.

Crickets jumped out of Josh's path as the crew pushed the cattle out of Waylon's pasture. The red-bodied bovines obeyed sluggishly, most still chewing their cud. Not a word had passed between Josh and Sol. The Prussian glanced warily at him from time to time but kept a fair distance. Overall, the crew worked wordlessly.

The horses more than made up for the men's lack of noise. Pocket whinnied frantically, afraid of being left behind. It had been agreed that the trapper would keep Pocket for the time being. Mary Ruth would doctor his sore hoof until Garret came back for him on the return trip. She held the end of his lead rope now.

The colt could not be made to stand still. Instead, Pocket jittered about, making his limp worse. Mary Ruth kept up with him, her expression quiet. She was not afraid of a bear, let alone a horse. She wore a fur coat such a light grey that it was almost white. Dew collected on her collar. Josh watched the dew drops touch her face. He glanced back again and again until he could no longer see the silver comb in her hair. Then, she faded out of sight.

Chapter Ten

The days trotted on uneventfully. Josh was glad to cover the miles without any major mishaps. Pepper had slipped into a steady rhythm and was responding to the lanky foreman's cues nicely. It was going to be a shame to see her go at the end of the drive. Selling the colts was always hard but it kept the ranch's circle of life running. The cycle had to keep moving to avoid becoming stagnant.

There was a change in Sol's expression. He still spoke very little unless spoken to but his eyes no longer darted around. He'd begun to let his reins sink around his saddle horn and wrap his fingers into the plain grey horse's mane as they rode. The horse turned out to have good cow-sense and flanked the herd without much instruction. Once, on his way to the back of the herd, Josh had caught Sol talking to the horse and noticed he called it Ramine.

Two day's ride past the trapper's home, the drive stopped near the mining camp of Bernice. The area made the hairs on Josh's neck stand on end, but his eyes couldn't find any cause for concern. Not willing to move camp just because his spine was crawling, Josh laid out his bedroll and waited for the feeling to pass. It didn't.

The cattle and horses were on edge about something too. Hofstede and Sol rode circles around the herd, trying to keep them together. Every few minutes, a handful of heifers would sneak past their watchmen and need to be retrieved. Even the cows who had eventually sat down still watched the tree line with suspicion.

Except for Hofstede's skinny mount, the horses usually stood ground tied through the night. Something about this place made them want to get away though. Every time Josh walked away from Old Bay, the big gelding would try to round up the other cow ponies and take off. The men were finally forced to tie all the horses to tree branches to keep them from running away.

In the middle of the night, Josh rose to take his shift watching the herd. He could still hear the herd's restlessness and figured he should wake another person to help him keep the cows together.

After a few solid nudges, Lincoln ceased his snoring. His breath reeked horribly when he finally sat up and asked, "Morning yet?"

"Night watch," Josh replied.

The trees cast long shadows all around them as Josh led Lincoln, still half-awake, past the dead cook fire. Restlessly stamping hooves alerted them that the cattle still hadn't settled down. If he strained his hearing, Josh could pick up Solomon's voice calling out a night herding song. The voice was cracked, unable to soothe itself, let alone the cattle.

Other noises abounded around the night. Josh welcomed the soft, eerie call of an owl. At least it was something familiar and explainable amidst all the uncomfortable shadows. Josh watched the trees as he walked, hoping to catch sight of the hooting bird, but as soon as the sound faded, it popped up more strongly in a different place. Despite the change, the owl never flew overhead. Josh decided there must be more than one owl. Nothing else could make that odd sound.

Josh stopped less than a yard away from the horses' tails. Old Bay eyed him, the whites around his pupils wide in the dark. The thud of the cattle reverberated through the earth. It didn't sound right. Lincoln, who hadn't been paying much attention, bumped into Josh's back. The men stood silently for a moment, listening.

The owl call rang out again, but this time a massive shadow appeared with it. The skin all across Josh's body crawled. His heart froze in his chest. The creature calling might have sounded like an owl, but it was not an owl that stood in front of them.

The horses sat back on their haunches, heels digging into the ground as they tried to pull away. Josh silently wished that he hadn't tied them with such strong ropes. The shadow-clad creature sniffed at the terrified horses, standing on its hind feet like a bear.

It scratched curiously at the tree that Pepper's lead rope was tied around. She froze, like a deer hoping a cougar wouldn't notice her. The beast began to utter a strange growl. Its massive teeth glared out. Pepper let out a terrible squeal and pulled back with all her might. The tree branch that she was tied to finally snapped. Splinters flew into the beast's face.

At that moment, Josh pulled his coat aside, reaching for his holstered pistol. Before he could get a handle on it, Lincoln leaped for the tree line, knocking him to the ground. Josh closed his eyes unintentionally. Air rushed by his face as the horse jumped over him, barely clearing his nose. The tree branch she dragged behind her slapped into his side, rolling him onto his stomach.

A smell like rotten fish filled Josh's lungs. He could hear the beast breathing. Without opening his eyes or aiming, the terrified foreman pulled the pistol's trigger. As soon as he could cock the gun again, Josh's eyes shot open. The creature was gone.

Ready to shoot at nothing, Josh scrambled to the trees. He found Lincoln trembling against a tall, slender tree trunk and crouched down next to him.

"Where is it?" Josh whispered.

Lincoln stared ahead blankly, frozen in shock.

Josh elbowed him solidly. "Where is the bear?"

"It's not a bear," Lincoln whimpered.

Trying to focus, Josh closed his eyes, listening for the thud of the monster's footsteps. The land was silent. "Stay here," he said, thrusting his pistol at Lincoln. "Shoot anything that's not a horse." He judged that he could make it back to camp in less than two minutes if he sprinted. Without waiting for Lincoln's okay, he took off running. His adrenaline carried him through the shadows until another gunshot rang out.

Garret kneeled at the edge of the camp; his rifle steadied on his knee. His shooting eye was level with the barrel. His chest held a deep, steady breath. He exhaled slowly, letting half of the air seep from his lungs, and pulled his trigger finger back until it released a bullet at his target. A great groan exploded out of the woods. "I got it that time," he said to Josh. "Let's go make sure it's dead."

"No, no, no" Josh sputtered. Nothing had ever sounded like a worse idea. "You're staying away from that thing."

In the dim starlight, Josh could see that Garret had terror in his eyes. Every one of the muscles in his body was tensed to keep them from trembling. Garret was just as afraid as anyone else, but the steady cowboy had no flight instinct, only fight.

"If it's dead, we're okay," Garret reasoned.

"Garret, that thing was bigger than a Grizzly, I don't think one bullet killed it."

"I got it in the head." His voice was unsure, so he added, "Plus, it was already limping."

"What if there's more than one?" Josh protested. He looked ahead at the tree line where Garret had shot. The maze of dark greenery was no place to wander into at night. "We're herding, not hunting," Josh decided. "We need to go find the horses and the others now."

Constantly glancing behind themselves, Josh and Garret collected Lincoln and the tied horses. They crept through the woods, wincing at every snapping twig. When they came upon the cattle herd, Josh's heart rate finally slowed.

Through some miracle, the herd was still all together. Some of the cattle even seemed to have calmed down. Josh found Pepper amid the cows, trembling violently. She still dragged the busted up tree branch. Using a pocket knife, Josh sawed her loose. Even then, she continued to shake.

All night, the crew guarded the edges of the herd. Their nerves still on edge; no one had trouble staying awake. Josh scheduled the men with guns, himself, Garret, and Hofstede, to let off a shot every so often. He hoped it would scare off anything else that lurked near. More than once, he shot at the imagined sound of a distant owl.

When the earliest light of dawn came, the men scrambled to pack up camp. Garret was finally allowed to check on the spot where he'd made his shot. Josh accompanied him if only to make sure he came back alive. The scene they found wasn't what they'd been expecting.

A faint impression of tracks crisscrossed the soggy ground between trees. The prints slipped into each other, making it impossible to tell how big they were or how many animals had made them. Though the men looked and looked for a carcass, they found none. Garret was finally able to locate a blood trail, proving at least one of their shots had met its mark.

Josh held his pistol ready as they followed the red specks. Every twig snapped by a squirrel made him look over his shoulder. Garret tracked the wounded beast's path until it ran into an impassable rock wall. Here, a massive indent, two inches deep and nine feet long, had crushed the earth.

"It bedded down here," Garret said. He took his rifle down off his shoulder as he crept forward.

Josh stood motionless. He carefully studied the rock wall, making sure there were no caves or crevices where a beast could hide. The wall was solid. It led thirty feet up into the sky above and spanned two hundred feet in either direction. He noticed that the red dots continued up the cliff when Garret nudged him.

Garret placed something heavy into Josh's free hand. The same smell of rotten fish rose from it. He stared down to find a wide, sharp tooth sitting in his palm. It was four or five times the size of a human canine. The shattered root still clung to it.

"Your shot must've grazed his cheek," Josh observed. He backed away from the wall quickly, suddenly afraid that something would appear at the top of the cliff.

"We need to get," Garret said.

The crew made a controlled stampede to cover the ground as quickly as possible. The cattle needed little encouragement to bolt down the trail. Even so, the men urged them on. Their horses moved between a high trot and a low gallop, eyes wide, nostrils flaring. It wasn't until they forded a low-running river and crossed into more open territory that the horses finally settled down.

For the first time in his life, Josh stopped the herd at noontime. In their scramble to get away from Bernice, the cowboys had skipped breakfast entirely. Their stomachs now growled, and Josh was in no humor to hear any more growling.

Garret cooked a double ration of beans that turned out halfway decent. The cowboys stretched out in the grass, sore and exhausted. Sol, in particular, was so stiff that he refused to get off of his horse. He claimed that if he did, he wouldn't be able to get back on. Garret laughed, pulled him down, and immediately looked a little sorry when the Prussian's numb legs collapsed. He hit the dirt with a thud.

Snoring soon filled the air. Even Josh slept through the noon hour. He judged they'd moved so fast over the morning that a short siesta couldn't put them behind schedule. There wasn't much of a choice anyway. Everyone's nerves were shot. Even closed, Josh's eyes twitched beneath his eyelids.

The foreman's body wasn't used to sleeping during the day, and he was the first to wake. One by one, the others awoke to the afternoon sun. Sol's threats proved meritless. He was able to climb back onto his horse when it was time for the drive to move on.

A few hours later, the drive crossed paths with a man wearing a silver badge who was riding south. Josh and Hofstede, who had been leading the herd, rode out to greet him. The trim, mustached man introduced himself as Sheriff Leo Tanner. He was fresh-faced despite claiming he had ridden from the Canadian border.

The sheriff ponied a second horse behind him that carried a prisoner handcuffed to the saddle horn. The outlaw sat rigidly in the saddle. He was a figure made of lean muscle and hatred. His eyes narrowed at Josh, and he muttered through the handkerchief gagging his mouth.

"This here's prisoner number one," Sheriff Tanner said, gesturing behind him. "He's got an appointment in Idaho that I'm taking him to." As an afterthought, he added, "He liked to talk too much."

"That's a long way," Josh said, impressed.

Sheriff Tanner shrugged. "It's where he'll stand trial."

Hofstede nodded his approval. "What's the varmint on trial for?" he chimed in.

"He stole a horse from a man, and that man died," the Sheriff answered.

In the remote west, horse theft was as good as murder. If a man didn't have quick enough means to make it between towns, he might not make it at all. With this being the case, a horse thief was the worst kind of criminal. Stealing a horse came with a price tag of a sure hanging if the thief was caught.

Hofstede shook his head. "I reckon he won't do that again."

"I'll make sure of it," Sheriff Tanner replied.

When the conversation lagged, Hofstede turned for the back of the herd. He was the only cowboy on the crew who refused to ride drag, but that seemed to be where he was going. Josh hoped he'd finally humbled himself a little. Soon, Garret trotted up the left of the herd, taking Hofstede's place.

The swatch of vast, open country between mountain ranges gave Josh a good chance to speak with the Sheriff. He strongly felt that his account of the monster Bernice was something that the law should hear. Perhaps the local deputy could trap it or at least drive it farther into the woods. The camp where they had been attacked was right on the only route through the area.

To Josh's surprise, when he described the nine foot tall, bear-like animal that could stand on its hind legs, Sheriff Tanner smiled at him.

"You're not going to try and scare me with that old ghost story, are you?" the sheriff laughed. "There's nothing in Bernice but miners."

Josh stared. Even the prisoner tied to the horse was rolling his eyes.

"Stories of a Bigfoot have come out of the Bernice mining camps for years," the Sheriff said. "Of course, there's nothing there. The miners figure that if they can scare everyone away, they'll get to keep all the gold."

"They're doing a good job," Josh said dryly.

Rather than argue with the Sheriff, Josh pulled the monstrous tooth out of his coat pocket.

"Are you sure there's nothing to it?" Josh said, pointedly.

Sheriff Tanner turned the tooth over in his hands. Doubt crossed his eyes for a moment. Then, he shook his head. "Yes, I'm sure, son," he chuckled. "That is a pretty good trinket though." He tossed the tooth back to Josh. "You got a claim up there you're trying to scare people off of?"

The Sheriff and his prisoner rode along with the herd for several more miles. Josh noted that when the outlaw's horse acted up, it was like it wanted to break free too. The stout buckskin gelding pulled back at least once every mile, digging his heels into the dirt and forcing the sheriff's horse to drag him for a few feet.

Eventually, Sheriff Tanner broke off from the cattle drive. He would be stopping in Butte for the night. There was a jailhouse there where the lawman could lock up his prisoner while he replenished supplies. Josh knew that if he

let his new hires into a Butte saloon, he would
never get them back out, so he wished the
lawman good luck and gave the town a wide
berth.

Chapter Ellevin

For days, clouds covered the sky as far as the eye could see. The wind roared, howled, and yipped between the sagebrush-covered gullies. Dry range grass offered itself, but Antelope and jackrabbits seemed to be the land's only owners.

Josh couldn't help but think that the scenery would be pretty if only he couldn't hear the wind. It battered mercilessly against his ears, giving him a constant headache. He pulled his hat brim down low, but it didn't do much to shield his stinging eyes. With straining resolve, he led the crew and cattle along the desolate miles. Nothing changed until a series of long, straight lines cut the horizon. Josh blinked hard, trying to make the image in front of him come into focus.

A five-strand barbwire fence stretched out in front of the trail. Josh had been here only a year ago, and as far as he knew, no one owned the land. It was barely more than useless. Still, there the fence was. A sturdy barrier around sagebrush and cheatgrass. He glanced left and right, but the barbwire followed the land down into gullies either direction. Its end wasn't in sight.

If someone in the group had been packing the necessary tools, they probably would have cut through the wire and patched it back together once the herd was through, but that wasn't the case. Josh strained his eyes, hoping to see a gate or a place that the fence was down. He rode west along the obstacle for a few minutes but had no such luck.

Without a better option, Josh turned the herd against the barbwire and used it to steer them west. They followed the fence for what seemed like hours. Without another soul in sight, Josh had begun to wonder if he was dreaming.

Garret rode up suddenly, snapping Josh out of his daze.

"We're wasting time. We need to get through this fence," Garret said.

Josh had jumped at the sudden voice. Pepper wheeled around to pin her ears at Garret's horse, bumping Josh's leg into the nearest cow.

"I agree, but I can't cut a fence with my bare hands," Josh replied. He reined Pepper in. "This fence can't go on forever," the foreman continued. Even as he said it, Josh doubted his own words. The five strands of taunt, tough barbwire guarded the landscape like a watchdog.

Garret raised his eyebrows skeptically in response. He didn't argue though. Instead, he set his horse into a trot, picking up the pace of the herd.

They followed the fence line up and down a series of gullies. Josh dug through his mind, trying to think of any way that he could break the barbwire. His hunting knife wouldn't touch the thick, twisted metal. Maybe there was something he could use to pry the nails loose from a post. The idea was gaining merit with him when he finally caught sight of a homestead in the foreground.

The outline of a house was still over a mile away at the edge of a flat, lonesome field. The fence stretched right up to it. A handful of skinny black and white milk cows grazed inside the enclosure. When they caught sight of the cowboys, the skittish Holsteins darted away. Josh shook his head. He couldn't imagine who would have fenced so much wasteland.

Eventually, the drive came up to homestead. For the first time in miles, a gate broke up the fence line. A stallion's scream greeted them. Josh studied the yard but couldn't see where the noise had originated.

He gave his crew the signal to wait while he approached the homestead's owner. He didn't want to stampede a herd of cattle through someone's yard unannounced.

Josh dismounted and looped the reins over his saddle horn, hoping his horse wouldn't wander. Staying ground-tied was new to her. The building's doorway stood void; its door ripped from the hinges. Dirt clung to the windows. The homestead looked abandoned.

A kitten played on the porch. At the sight of Josh, it darted underneath a hole in the firewood pile. The kitten's yellow eyes peered out at him as the foreman approached the house.

He was afraid to find someone inside. Considering the condition of the place, he was nervous that some disaster might have happened here. Leaving a perfectly good house was peculiar. Perhaps that meant someone hadn't been able to leave.

It took a moment for Josh's eyes to adjust when he stepped across the threshold. Dust particles floated in the stale air. The homestead was empty. Josh sighed, relieved. It was void of dishes, clothes, and home goods. Whoever had wasted their time on the fence must have already moved on.

In a few strides, Josh crossed the empty house and reaffirmed that there wasn't a single object inside. Cobwebs collected in the corners. Sunbeams spilled in through the windows, showcasing the dust on the floorboards. Josh turned to leave, retracing the prints his boots had made by disturbing the dirt.

When Josh emerged from the abandoned house, Garret was holding Pepper by the reins.

"I think she was going for that stud that's been calling," Garret said. As if on cue, the high, eerie, scream of a stallion pierced the air again.

Pepper's ears flicked forward. She danced about excitedly. Josh swung up onto the filly's back and let the reins drape loosely. Without interference from her rider, Pepper followed the stallion's call, carrying Josh around the homestead to a tightly built corral system.

Josh quickly counted up the band of horses left behind in the corrals. One stallion, four mares, and a small colt. The stud was tall- at least sixteen hands- and big-boned though his ribs shown through his dirty white coat. He perched his head on top of the highest wooden rail and stared out at Pepper. He raised his lip, smelling the air, and whinnied again.

The horses were painfully skinny. Their enclosure might have had three weeks' worth of grazing in it at one point but they'd long since picked it clean, and the earth was now barren. The mares poked around the dirt, begging it to give up even a tiny weed. Teeth marks on the rough-cut corral showed where they had been gnawing off the bark for something to chew on.

The horses were pitiful but it was the sight the other side of the homestead made Josh's heart sink. The barbwire fence picked right back up and continued indefinitely. As far as the eye could see, fence posts grew out of the ground. Five tight strands guarded the homestead as if there was something of value there to protect. The foreman stared at the horizon, wishing the fence would disintegrate. Suddenly, Josh heard Garret shout behind him.

"We're saved, boys!" Garret yelled. He waved a pair of fence cutters in the air, grinning triumphantly. The ecstatic cowboy tossed the tool to Josh. "Look what I found lying around!"

"It's our own little miracle," Josh replied. He turned to look over the landscape. "Do you think we should ride back west to where we started this morning? We've gone pretty far off course."

"If we cut through the fence here and keep going, we'll just come out on the other side of Moose Creek," Garret suggested.

Josh pondered the idea, running a map in his mind's eye. "We're cutting the fence," he announced.

It didn't take long to chop a section of fence down and funnel the tired heifers through it. Josh led the way, as usual, followed by Lincoln and Sol. Garret was stuck bringing up the rear with Hofstede, which gave them a few more minutes to look around. However, there wasn't much to see. The place was sterile except for an oversized role of barbwire and several stacks of unused fence posts. Garret slumped forward with his hands in his pockets and watched Hofstede wander through the post piles.

"Not much here," Garrett commented.

"What about them?" Hofstede asked, gesturing to the corralled nags. "We could sell them cheap and still make a dollar. No doubt some soft-hearted lady would take them off our hands."

Garret's eyes narrowed. "We can't just take them." The horses were thin, but they weren't dead, which meant that the owner hadn't been absent long. "Whoever lives here might need them when they come back."

"Okay, not all of them," Hofstede decided. "I'm mostly concerned about the stallion," His eyes were rotating around a plan. "He's worth more than all the rest. That'd more than make up for the bonus we're losing for being late with the cattle."

"We're not late yet," Garret snapped.

"Consider it insurance money then." Hofstede readied a lariat to catch the white stud.

"You forgot this place isn't ours," Garret said as he placed himself in between Hofstede and the corral gate. There was a look on Hofstede's face that Garret didn't like.

"It's abandoned property!" Hofstede snarled.

Garret, stroked his chin, feeling the stubble that had grown in from the days on the trail. "Go talk it over with Josh," he finally said.

Hofstede mounted his horse as quickly as he could and galloped off.

Standing alone by the abandoned horses made Garret feel like he'd been abandoned himself. He peered between the fence rails to study the nags. Through a layer of mud, Garret could see they were branded with a large capital letter Q on the left hip. There wasn't anything very distinctive about the mares. The colt's face resembled the stallion. He was pitch black, which at this age meant he would probably fade to grey and then white as he aged.

Garret never had much intention of waiting for Josh's response. They'd been working together for long enough that he knew what the answer would be. As soon as the tail of Hofstede's horse was out of sight, Garret wrapped a hand around the wooden gate. The stallion snorted, pawing at the dirt. Garret tightened his grip on Missy Lew's reins before he swung the gate wide open.

The stallion exploded out of the corral. All four mares followed in a flash. The colt, however, didn't know how to find the exit. He'd probably never been outside the pen before.

The terrified foal ran blindly, his legs coiling up beneath him as he galloped, smashing into the wooden rails. A fresh gouge appeared on his black face. Garret tried to stand back, but he soon couldn't stand watching the fiasco anymore.

In one fluid motion, Garret got on his horse, threw a loop around the colt's neck, and dallied on to the saddle horn. The black colt pulled back against the rope that confined him. Garret wanted to get this over with quickly. He used Missy Lew's weight to drag the reluctant rescue case outside and pulled him close to take the lariat off. The colt's new head wound didn't look too bad up close. It must have hurt, but it would heal on its own. Garret guessed that it would leave a scar.

Once he was free, the black stud colt stood dazed. Garret waved a hand to shoo him away, but he stared, unblinking. Garret smiled and shook his head. Missy Lew wasn't as amused. She pinned her ears, threatening to bite. When the young horse eventually came back to his senses, his stumpy black tail flew out behind him, and he raced to rejoin his herd.

Garret had moved the last heifer through the gap in the fence and had three of the five barbwire strands patched up by the time Hofstede reappeared. The man's expression radiated hate. He'd clearly gotten a resounding no from Josh. Garret could barely stop himself from smirking.

As he climbed back in the saddle, Garrett caught sight of the feral horses running wildly within the miles of barbwire fence. The broad cowboy got to hear Hofstede cussing under his breath for the next hour or so, but he felt like he'd made the right move.

With the abandoned homestead behind them, the cowboys continued south. What they'd never known was that riding the wrong side of Moose Creek meant cutting through land that was almost a marsh. Tall, slender aspen trees covered the ground for acres. Guiding the cattle through the aspens was incredibly slow work. The men had to duck and dodge every thirty seconds to avoid being hit by a branch.

Josh did his best to hurry the cattle along, starting as early as he could see and continuing until dark. The cowboys obeyed, though Hofstede and Lincoln did so grudgingly. Detouring from the road had cost them. The deadline for reaching the train was now only a day away. Worse yet, the clouds were broadcasting a darker hue with every mile. They were running short on time.

The Chinook wind blew wild and strong, and Kaitlyn embraced it, hair flying, chilled to the bone. She peered into the storm, hoping against all odds to see a lantern's glow. The cattle drive should have arrived by now. Straining her ears, the schoolteacher listened for the sound of hooves. She would have never been able to hear them above the storm, but she listened anyway.

Kaitlyn soon realized she was doing no good standing outside. She resigned herself to the schoolhouse. If the cattle drive somehow found their way, they might arrive frozen half to death, so she set about building a fire in the schoolhouse. Just as a spark ignited the kindling Kaitlyn had put in the stove, rain escaped the heavy clouds. The schoolteacher paced the building until she wound up at the window.

The thin window was an inadequate buffer against the cold and Kaitlyn leaned close against it, letting it freeze her bones. The chill was crisp on her skin. Goosebumps rose on her arms but she didn't shiver. It felt like the cold somehow connected her to her friends who were likely lost somewhere in it.

She peered out at Dolly. The mare stood slumped under the protection of the overhang with a hind hoof cocked, her black mane taking flight in the wind. Through the glass, Kaitlyn thought she could see Dolly's heart hurting, longing to be in some other horse's life, somewhere else.

Chapter Twelve

The rising sun stretched orange and pink layers of color over a dewy sky just in time for the Heide Ranch cattle drive to reach the outskirts of Dillon. Behind him, Josh could hear the cowboys hoopin' and hollerin' about their victory. Josh remained stoic, but he felt the relief of a heavy responsibility lifting from his shoulders. Breathing was suddenly significantly easier.

It was a straight shot down Main Street to the Jonathan B. Wylie stockyard and railroad station. The town was still quiet except for a small woman carrying goods from the bakery to the Longhorn. The Herefords had free reign of the street. A few of them jumped up to the boardwalk for a better view. Josh tossed his rope at a heifer who was transfixed with her reflection in a store window. She sent a kick sideways at the lariat, skittered away, and rejoined the herd.

Meanwhile, Kaitlyn awoke to find herself away from her bed. The teacher had fallen asleep on a pile of Navajo blankets in the schoolroom. Huddled next to the fire, the rain, and then eventually hail, on the roof had lulled her to sleep. Seeing the light pour in through the windows made her scramble to her feet. She raced to the door and stepped outside just in time to look at the tails of a few reluctant Herefords reaching the railroad yard.

Kaitlyn shouted excitedly, unconcerned if anyone saw her. She had run halfway across the schoolyard before she remembered she wasn't wearing any shoes. She looked down at the dry dirt clinging between her toes and smiled at her mistake. On second thought, maybe it was worth taking a few minutes to fix her tangled hair and wrinkled dress. She bounded back inside.

On the south end of town, Josh sat with his hat in his hand. It was a darker brown than it had been at the beginning of the drive. Miles of trail dirt had found their way into the felt. He picked at the dirt particles nervously. William Hofstede sat beside him, just as tense.

Across the mahogany business desk, Mr. Wylie Continued. "Surely you're not going to trail these heifers clear back to Butte just to make a few cents more per pound," Wylie said. "It would be a waste of time." He tapped the ash off his cigar. "Six dollars a hundredweight. That's my best offer."

Josh's throat was dry. The foreman reached into his coat and pulled out a folded up flyer. He smoothed it out on the table and pushed it towards Wylie with a stiff hand.

"You're advertising a lot more than that," Josh muttered. "I was hoping for at least a hundred per head." He stared down at the wrinkled paper. The upside down lettering seemed to be mocking him.

"That price is for premium cattle," Wylie explained.

"Premium cattle," Josh mumbled under his breath.

"That flyer doesn't say six dollars!" Hofstede interrupted. How did a hundred bucks a cow turn into, what does that come to? Eighty bucks a head?" The new hire was suddenly very invested in the ranch's interests.

Wylie seemed unaffected. He reached into a desk drawer. Without making eye contact, the businessman counted out a chunk of crisp handbills and put them in an unembellished leather wallet. He whistled while he recounted the bills and snapped the wallet closed.

"Consider this a down payment," he said. "I'm confident that you'll change your mind by shipping time in the morning." He passed the wallet towards Josh. It sat on the table, untouched.

"How do you know we won't split with the money?" Hofstede asked.

"Where would you run to with a big herd of cattle?" Wylie replied. He seemed genuinely amused. "Cows slow you down. If a man tried to escape with my money and a full herd, I'd have him strung up in less than a day." He shook his head and took another puff of his cigar.

Josh stood up abruptly. "Those are the best cattle in the state!" He shouted. "Maybe in the whole West." His hands were trembling. "If they're not worth premium price then nothing is!"

He towered over Wylie's office desk, and for a moment Josh felt like he could have pounded J.B. Wylie straight into the ground like a fence post. The feeling must have shone through Josh's eyes because the crook shrunk bank in his leather armchair. Josh pulled the wooden door open so violently that it slammed against the wall. He had stormed halfway down the block and nearly ran over Garret before either of the other men in the room had moved.

Hofstede stared down at the leather wallet. It was more money than he'd seen in one place in a long time. Not nearly what the cows were worth, but still a sizable chunk of wealth. He hesitated. "I'm sure we can all talk this over," he finally said.

Kaitlyn flew the length of Dillon's main street in a moment. Dolly's hooves covered the hard-packed dirt, barely touching down. Kaitlyn stood in her stirrups, her heart exploding with a sensation she couldn't explain. Before Dolly fully stopped, she leaped out of the saddle into Garret's waiting embrace.

He twirled her in a circle, boots high off the ground. When she returned to earth, Josh's towering figure bent down to quickly hug her shoulders. His lanky arms made her feel like a child, but it was a feeling she didn't mind. It was wonderful to feel childlike, standing with her old friends again. She stepped back, beaming. The only thought that came to mind was, "home." Finally. Now, she'd be able to go home.

Garret gave her a hard look. "You don't look like a school teacher to me," he teased.

Kaitlyn tried to scowl at him, but it lasted half a second. She couldn't stop smiling.

"Yeah, are school teachers supposed to wear riding skirts?" Josh chimed in.

Kaitlyn laughed. "Well, what do I look like then?" she asked.

Josh and Garret glanced at each other, silently consulting.

"You look like a runaway booking it down the street on your horse," Garret teased.

"I wish!" Kaitlyn laughed. "How is it that you can already tell I'm not quite in love with this town?"

"Well, I've never seen Dolly go that fast before," Josh said. "I thought you'd just keep going past us and we'd see you back at the ranch."

"The ranch is that way," Kaitlyn said, gesturing over her shoulder. She raised an eyebrow sarcastically. "He's in charge of navigating?" she joked.

"Yes, it's a wonder we're not in Canada," Garret answered.

"Hold on, now. I got us here, didn't I?" Josh said, trying to defend himself.

"Barely," Garret laughed.

Kaitlyn watched the boys bantering. They were covered in trail dust and scruffy from days on the drive, but she thought they looked like heroes, come to save the day.

Garret turned to her again. "What do you say?" he asked. "We can make you the runaway schoolteacher. Come back with us." His dark green eyes were wide, expecting an honest answer.

Just then, Judd and Jeremiah Wylie's matching sorrels came trotting around the corner. The boys couldn't have made them go in a straight line if they'd tried, so the large horses zigzagged down the street, nearly trampling the town's few early-rising pedestrians.

They made a wide arc around either side of Kaitlyn and her companions, staring at the men's ragged appearance. As they passed, thoughts of what might happen if they got to the schoolroom first flashed through Kaitlyn's mind. She pictured pages torn out of math books and mischievously placed inside Bibles or all of the desks stacked up to block the front door.

"I'd better find you again and talk later," she said hurriedly.

Garret nodded. "We'll be at the Longhorn trying to get some colts sold," he said.

Kaitlyn swung up onto Dolly. The teacher had started for the school when she heard Josh failing to conceal a laugh behind her. She looked back over her shoulder to see Darla had finally given up on kicking her new pony and was leading, or rather dragging it through town. The spectacle was a tug-of-war that Darla seemed to be losing. Every time she made a few hard-fought steps forward, the pony's head would shoot down to some tiny skiff of grass in the street. Then Darla would have to haul with all the might to pry the pony's stubborn muzzle off the ground.

Taking pity on her, Garret called out, "Do you need some help there, little miss?"

Darla whirled around, startled. Her blue eyes were wide. She was wise enough to know better than to talk to strangers. It looked like she was considering running for the nearest storefront and abandoning her immobile pony, so Kaitlyn stepped in.

"It's alright, Darla," she shouted. Kaitlyn rode the short distance between them and continued. "It's okay. These are my friends."

Darla smiled, suddenly changing her mind about the offer for help. Josh looked on, still chuckling, while Garret grabbed ahold of the pony's reins. The sluggish creature knew instantly that someone with more authority had taken charge. He raised his head obediently and gave Garret a guilty, somewhat apologetic look.

"Here, hand me the reins and I'll lead her," Kaitlyn offered.

Garret handed up the reins, giving the pony a stern look of warning. He knelt next to Darla. "Would you like help?" he asked. Darla stared up at him, her eyes wide again.

The little girl's, "yes," was so tiny that it wasn't audible but she nodded her head.

Garret scooped her up into the saddle, patted her on the back, and smiled at Kaitlyn. "She's all yours," he said. "Away you go."

Chapter Thirteen

The inside of the Longhorn Saloon had changed since Josh had last been a customer. He'd never been in town at the proper time to see the breakfast ensemble. The tables went without their decor, unadorned except for freshly filled salt and pepper shakers. Plenty of the previous night's mess was still leftover, including a corner that boasted the broken remains of a whiskey glass and a puddle of vomit that none of the staff seemed willing to acknowledge.

Josh chose the table farthest from the offending corner and motioned for Garret to join him. The waiter brought them two glasses of water immediately, which they both ignored. Plain tan coffee cups sat upside down in the center of the table. The men flipped their cups right-side up and slid them to the corner of the table.

When the waiter came around again to pour their coffee and Josh picked up his full cup, he noticed that his hands still hadn't entirely stopped shaking. He endured three large gulps of black coffee so that there would be enough room to put sufficient heavy cream into the mix. Then he sat back in his chair and stared blankly at his companion.

Garret had bargained with Wylie to keep the heifers corralled for the day. It bought them some time to think. With no sleep the previous night to speak of, there might not be much thinking going on even with an extra day dedicated to it. The men drank their coffee, both thankful to the other for not yet breaking the silence.

When a plate of fresh bacon and scrambled eggs appeared in front of him, Garret finally found the energy to speak. "I think Wylie's bluffing," he said.

Josh, whose food hadn't arrived yet, shook his head.

"I'm telling you, he's playing chicken with us," Garret insisted.

Josh's glazed eyes stared down at Garret's plate. He moved his hand forward slowly, pointing to a piece of bacon.

Garret's eyes narrowed. "Wait for your own," he said.

"I got fried steak," Josh replied. "Probably why it's taking so long."

Garret rolled his eyes. "You're like a woman," he said, throwing the smallest bacon strip onto Josh's napkin.

"How would you know?" Josh mumbled. He picked up his bacon quickly, not wanting to lose it over a cheap joke.

Garret's expression turned into a glare. He drank his coffee indignantly.

Finally, Josh's plate came. He was halfway through it almost the instant it touched the table. He asked the waiter for an extra side of hash browns and wasted no time letting the eggs cool down. When his stomach started to reach the half-full point, he felt revived enough to address their predicament.

"He wasn't bluffing," Josh said. "He was dead serious. You should have been at that meeting. It was either sell to him cheap or keep on moving down the road."

"I can't imagine he's that foolish," Garret replied. "He can tell those are nice cows. He's just putting on a poker face."

"I think other folks have all been giving in to his poker face," Josh cut in. "He's pretty used to getting his way by now."

Garret fidgeted with his crumpled up napkin. "This is a fine mess," he muttered.

"I tell you what," Josh said. "I'm giving Wylie until the end of the day to up his offer. If he doesn't do it, I'm trailing the beeves back to Butte and selling them there."

Eventually, Garret nodded slowly. Butte's market wasn't going to give them the money they'd been expecting to get in Dillon, but it was a matter of principle at this point. Wylie's flyers had been a scam. They'd gone an extra sixty miles for his advertised price. Now, if Wylie didn't give in, it had all been for nothing.

"I'm going to ask around for anyone looking to buy a horse," Josh continued. "You might as well go have a look at the rest of the town."

There was a small Chinese Laundry nook down the street from the Longhorn. It housed a bathing facility in the back that charged patrons a quarter to wash up. While Josh took his turn manning the horse sales, Garret headed straight for the wash basins.

An awkward looking boy took Garret's twenty-five cents and, after inspecting it, showed him back to a sort of wash stall. It was spacious and clean with a smooth wooden bench to sit on. There was even a perfectly sanded shelf holding a still-wrapped bar of soap. Garret sat down and removed his boots while the boy retrieved two massive pitchers full of clean water.

"Careful. Very hot," the boy said in high pitched broken English.

"That'll be alright," Garret mused. He gestured to his stained shirt and dirty jeans. "Can you wash these for me?" he asked.

"Yes, yes ten cent," the boy replied. He continued to rush back and forth, carrying large laundry baskets.

Garret latched the stall door and peeled off his cattle drive clothes. Standing in bare feet was a foreign feeling after so many days spent in boots. Relieved, he tossed his dirty wardrobe over the stall door for the boy to collect. The cowboy sat down on the bench and let his tensed muscles relax.

With so many days' worth of dirt, it was hard to know where to begin. Garret pulled down one of the large pitchers and tested its temperature. A thin puff of steam wafted into the air. The rest of the water gravitated to a clever drain in the middle of the stall floor.

Tilting the pitcher over his head, Garret let the contents run out all at once like a waterfall. Pasty tan trail dirt drizzled down off of his chin. He rinsed and lathered his hair several times, scooping his hands back through the dark mop to pull any residual dirt out. By the time he'd used all of his allotted water and called for more, he was beginning to feel more man than mud.

When enough water and time had passed, Garret began to think about the state of his facial hair. Usually, the trail's end was an occasion to visit a proper barber. This time was different though. With no money coming in for the cows, there was no telling when he'd be getting paid. Garret decided he'd better be careful with what money he had.

He'd seen a mirror in the corner of the room that would suffice for shaving. Garret pulled down a towel that the Chinese boy had thrown over the door for him. He unfolded it, disappointed to find out there wasn't very much to the cloth. He dried off the best he could, but the towel was much too small to fit around his waist.

"I need a bigger towel," he said, throwing it at the boy. The worker's mouth was aghast. It looked annoyingly dumb. "Another towel," Garret repeated. The short figure dashed out of the room. While he stood there waiting, Garret dug through the bundle he'd brought to town with him.

On his way to finding a straight razor, he came across a pair of grey cotton underwear and a bright red shirt. The ranch hand had saved these so he would have something clean to wear when Kaitlyn came to dinner. He resented the fact he'd only brought one pair of pants, which the Chinaman was now washing. Garret pulled the fresh underwear on and laid the red shirt out, smoothing its wrinkled sleeves. The young cowboy felt like a new man. He even found a clean pair of socks, which he threw in one of his boots.

When the Chinese boy returned, he was holding a towel in one hand and a sharp, short garden spade in the other. Garret raised his eyebrows, trying not the laugh at the kid's peculiar expression. He held his hand out for the towel. The worker inched towards him, hand outstretched. "Strange fella," Garret muttered under his breath. He grabbed the towel roughly.

Standing close to the boy, Garret noticed a long, beaded necklace for the first time. It seemed too feminine for a boy to be wearing. Suddenly, Garret's cheeks turned very red. He realized that the Chinese boy wasn't a boy at all but a shapeless, short-haired woman.

He, who was, in fact, she, stared at him wide-eyed. She rushed out of the room quickly. Garret tried to laugh, but the embarrassment was still too fresh. Figuring she wouldn't come back, he attempted to

shave with what water he had left. He
desperately hoped that his pants would be
ready soon.

The cowboy had been correct in
assuming that the Chinese woman would not
be returning. Instead, an angry voice, this one
distinctly male, flew down the hallway.

"You want wife you get own wife!" The
voice proceeded its owner, a mustached
Chinaman who was toting a rifle that was
almost as big as him.

Garret's mouth went dry. He'd always
imagined he'd die in a heroic gun fight, a
stampede, or a historical war battle. Being
killed in his underwear in a Chinese bathhouse
wasn't on the list.

"There's been a mistake," Garret
managed. "I just wanted to shave."

The Chinaman's lip curled up in a snarl.
He pointed his gun.

"Oh, dear Glory No" Garret gasped. He waved his arms, realizing the man didn't speak any English.

"This not brothel!" the mustached man screeched. Including a pointy hat, he barely came up to Garret's shoulder. That was little comfort when the offended Chinese worker had a clear shot.

With his hands in the air, Garret backed towards the door. "I'm sorry. Um, misunderstanding." He was trying to come up with another way to plead when his bare feet hit the dirt of the street. He turned on his heel and ran full force for the alleyway. The Chinaman didn't follow.

It was Garret's good fortune to find his pants hanging on a clothesline behind the Chinese laundry. His work shirt, however, had been thrown outside to be trampled into the dirt. He had to walk barefoot through town to find the other crew members. Both Hofstede and Lincoln were already too drunk to care much about Garret's account. Sol, however, was still reasonably sober.

With some work, Garret eventually convinced Sol to retrieve his belongings from inside the laundry nook. Though the Chinese couple gave the clothes and boots back willingly, Josh wasn't about to take the risk of a repeat incident, leaving a hotel on the other end of town as his last resort for a wash. Since the place was known to be a brothel, he couldn't sit down anywhere for fear of catching some terrible itch. Josh emerged only halfway clean and completely disgruntled.

Lincoln, Hofstede, and unfortunately Sol, who smelt the worse out of all of them, didn't care much about washing up. After doing Garret's bidding, Sol had wandered off. The others had set up camp inside the Longhorn. Lincoln and Hofstede's patronage to the bar was significant enough that the owner agreed to let Josh take up the entire hitching rail. He asked for an old piece of scrap wood and painted it with the words, "FOR SALE: Nice Ranch Horses. $200.00 to $220.00. Ask Inside." Josh hung his sign by the tied up colts and waited.

In the Longhorn's candlelight, Josh looked older. Fine creases were starting to appear around his light brown eyes. Kaitlyn absentmindedly pinned an escaped curl while the pair waited for Garret to arrive. She realized that she'd entirely forgotten how to talk to Josh. Her offers at small talk went largely unreturned. She sipped her tea, settling into awkward silence.

"How were your colts this year?" she asked, making one more attempt to strike a conversation.

Josh lit up. "Oh they were great," he replied. "That black filly is just like Dolly. She was hard to figure out."

"They're sensitive horses," Kaitlyn agreed.

"Once I figured Daisy out I liked her, though," Josh added. "Dolly must have been pretty difficult too."

"Grandma had to help me with her a lot," Kaitlyn admitted.

Kaitlyn glanced up to see Garret's figure walking through the restaurant. He had regained his dignity from earlier in the day and now strode with his usual confidence. His rescued red shirt was accompanied by a silver bolo tie that flickered in the candlelight.

"Two colts sold," he announced. "One feller was so excited he paid for Missy Lew today." He patted his pocket, grinning.

"That's pretty good!" Kaitlyn exclaimed.

Garret pulled out a chair and sat next to Josh. He smiled at Kaitlyn warmly. "Would you take one-ninety for Daisy?" he asked.

Kaitlyn laughed. "They're not my horses!" she exclaimed. "Ask Josh."

"Who's offering?" Josh inquired, leaning in.

"It's a cowboy who works for Wylie." Garret replied, "Good guy though."

"Figures one of Wylie's guys would be trying to bargain," Josh scoffed.

Kaitlyn swallowed nervously, but it went unnoticed. "One ninety's not bad," she noted. "She's still pretty green, and with things going the way they are it might be best to take what you can get."

In response, Josh sighed deeply. Kaitlyn looked on with some pity. The foreman had already filled her in on the day's events. Wylie still hadn't budged on his lowball offer. Wylie's scam was a disappointment to her but sadly enough, hearing about it wasn't a surprise. She retreated into her thoughts, wondering what she'd seen in the conman.

Eventually, Josh conceded on Daisy's price. He had more pressing issues to see to than ten dollars. On that list was a double portion of mashed potatoes that he'd just started eating. The trio spoke between bites for well over an hour. They decided that it was best to trail the cattle back to Butte and sell them there. Josh agreed, with some hesitation, that it was best for Kaitlyn to ride with the drive if she planned on coming home to the ranch. She would send her belongings ahead on a supply stage that went as far as Helena.

When the meal and pie were gone, even Josh was full. He took care of the tab, meeting Garret and Kaitlyn at the door. Though the sun had long since set, the street was full of moonlight. Down the road, Kaitlyn could see that the stockyard was nearly empty.

"Where are the heifers?" she asked, turning to Josh.

"The boys are holding them out on the plain north of town," Josh explained.

"It took a cold bucket of water to sober Lincoln up enough, but he got on his horse," Garret laughed.

Josh rolled his eyes. "We'll go relieve him of his hard work for the night."

"It's too late to ride out there tonight" Kaitlyn protested. "It's all full of cactus and gopher holes. Stay here. There's plenty of space by the fire for your bedrolls."

"Aren't you worried about what people will say?" Garrett joked. "You're having two good looking men stay the night. The little old Betties will have a gossip fest."

"You're not funny," Kaitlyn informed him.

"Then why are you laughing?" Garret asked.

Josh shook his head. "Knock it off."

While Kaitlyn ran ahead to get a fire going, the boys untied Old Bay and Pepper from the Longhorn's hitching rail. They led their horses down the street, too saddle sore to be interested in mounting up for such a short ride. A strong wind gusted through the town, pushing them along.

Chapter Fourteen

The night was nearly as bright as dawn with the full moon illuminating the landscape. Hofstede sat in the dirt counting out a deck of cards that he always carried in his coat pocket. Two extra aces- club and heart- stayed pinned inside his sleeve. Hofstede gave the cards a final shuffle. His eyes darted about in agitation as he slipped them back into his pocket.

Lincoln was somewhere at the opposite end of the camp nursing a flask of whiskey while his horse dozed underneath him. Sol rode circles around the herd singing loudly in an off-key vice that irritated the men much more than it soothed the cattle. His words drifted in and out of nonsense as he invented new lyrics to an old cowboy melody.

Silver Moon in Montana.
That's where you will find me
With my few good companions

Sol finished his round just in time to find Hofstede angrily tossing gravel into two different piles. It was an odd sight to see a grown man sitting in the dirt, throwing rocks. He was ripping small stones out of the grass one or two at a time to keep count of something. There seemed to be a flawed method to it. He muttered very loudly, cursing this number or that as he added to his own frustration. He clearly didn't like Sol's questioning stare.

"I'm trying to find out how much this old man is ripping me off for my work!" Hofstede yelled.

Turning his back, he continued counting out gravel pebbles. "I'm being took!" he spat. "Come all the way down here, and now there's no payout! The kid wants us to go all the way back to another speck of a cow town just to get paid!"

"Well," Sol stammered, "Josh'll give us our day wages now if we leave. He can just hire other men in town." His words fell on deaf ears.

Hofstede pointed to his two stone piles on the ground, one towering over the other. "Look! That's how much these cattle are worth altogether," he explained, spreading his arms out to cup his hands around both piles. Then he poked a finger at the small pile "That's how much pay I'm getting out of the deal!" he snuffed.

Something about this accounting method didn't seem right to Sol, and it wasn't just the fact that it was done with gravel. He spent a few moments trying to count up the stacked petals in the moonlight but quickly gave up.

"What about Lincoln and me?" he asked.

"Oh you're in there" Hofstede growled. "Your money's in the big pile."

"Why don't we get our own piles?"

"I'm not counting for you. I'm counting for me" Hofstede rose to his feet and spat out the tobacco he'd been working over.

"Course, there is a way I could count you in," he continued. The light in his eyes had changed. His eyebrows scrunched down while he thought. The thinking process was slow for Hofstede, not because he was stupid but because he liked to weigh his options carefully.

In the silence, Sol found a rock to sit on and stared up at the full moon. There was a pretty good chance Hofstede would decide to leave Sol out of his proposition. Whatever it was, Sol desperately hoped that would be the case. The last thing he wanted was to challenge Josh's plans on behalf of Hofstede.

"I think I'll keep going with the Heide outfit," Sol thought out loud. "It's only a few more days to the next train yard, and we could make it alright with Josh and Garrett and me."

Hofstede didn't acknowledge a word Sol had said. Both of the men were muttering out their own plans when Lincoln's wobbly form appeared nearby. He slipped off his horse, who seemed relieved to be rid of him. Lincoln was steadier on the ground than he had been horseback. He approached Hofstede expectantly. They already knew something that Sol didn't.

"That Wylie fellow is offering us good money for these beeves, and we're just leaving it all on the table," Hofstede said.

"It's hardly any good," Sol piped up. "These heifers are worth a lot more than a lousy eighty dollars each."

Hofstede continued to talk right over top of him, "My boy, we're going to do right by Mr. Wylie. He was expecting enough cattle to fill his shipment, and we're going to make sure he gets them."

"We're keeping the money too" Lincoln announced.

Hofstede looked over, annoyed. "You drunk! Did you have to go and spoil the whole plan?"

"I'm keeping mine," Lincoln replied.

"Yes, you keep your share," Hofstede humored. "You," he said, turning to Sol, "Could have a pretty little share for your efforts too. It's just one night's work. We drive these cattle down to the train yard, split the money from Wylie, and head out of town."

Sol's face went pale. "How are you going to head out of town without a fast horse?" He said. "In case you forgot, that quarter-mile pony you've been borrowing belongs to Mr. Heide."

"Finders keepers," Hofstede laughed. "Those boys don't need extra horses if they don't have cattle to push!" Lincoln joined in a deep guttural laugh, but Sol was silent.

"No," The word was almost a whisper. Sol wasn't sure it had come from him, but it had.

Hofstede's expression turned cold. "What did you say?" he asked.

"No! No, not me. Horse thieves get hung, and I'm not getting hung." This time, Sol was sure the words had come from his own mouth. "I'm not a cattle rustler either!" he yelled. "And I ain't stealing from good men for the likes of you!"

Hofstede's eyes bulged with rage. He grabbed Sol by the collar and raised his long-time partner a foot off the ground, bringing them eye-level. Hofstede threw Sol back with all his might. Sol landed hard, knocking the wind out of his chest. He gasped for air, the shocked expression on his face turning white.

Lincoln stood by, waiting to pounce. Once Sol was down, the half-drunk cowboy closed in, kicking savagely at his exposed ribs. He smirked wickedly, kicking like his victim was only a mound of dirt in his way. Once Sol regained his senses, he rolled onto his side, leaving Lincoln's hard-toed boots to crack into his backbone. The scrawny man knew if he was going to have any chance, he had to get back up and fast.

Sol twisted onto his stomach and reached out. Lincoln's reflexes were slow from lubricating his throat with whiskey for the last two hundred miles. Sol hooked his arm around his attacker's knee and yanked hard. Lincoln crashed to the ground. In a blur, Sol untangled himself and scrambled to his feet. The frantic cowboy began running almost before he had fully stood and well before he had decided where he was running to.

A nicker from nearby caught Sol's attention as he sprinted aimlessly. His grey gelding, Ramine, was picketed at the edge of the clearing. The gelding stared inquisitively at the scene unfolding in the camp. His great brown eyes met Sol's and both filled with sheer terror. Ramine began to prance back and forth, testing the picket as Sol raced towards him.

Sol didn't dare look back. He could hear the rapid sound of footsteps chasing behind him. Their spurs clanged like war armor as his pursuers closed the gap between them. Just as Sol reached Ramine, the horse pulled back with all his strength. The picket ripped out of the ground. Sol leaped as high as he could and swung a leg over the gelding's back. He clung to Ramine's mane, hanging off the horse's side. Ramine had no intentions of waiting for Sol to situate himself. The horse took off, dragging the picket behind him.

Miraculously, Sol was able to wiggle the rest of the way up onto the horse's back as they bolted away. The Prussian saw the steel picket bouncing along behind them and knew it wouldn't be long before it caught on a rock or sagebrush bush, cutting off their escape. He was by no means an excellent rider. It took all of his strength to keep his trembling legs wrapped around the giant horse while he dug in his pocket for a knife. Leaning low onto the horse's neck, Sol reached down and sawed off most of the lead rope off. Now that he at least had one rein, he steered Ramine towards Dillon. If he made it to the edge of town, he could warn Josh and Garret before it was too late.

Suddenly, a rapid whooshing sound filled Sol's ears. There was no time to react. The loop of a lariat tightened around his neck like a boa constrictor. He saw nothing but grassland, then the moonlit sky, then complete darkness.

Chapter Fifteen

A loud bang in the late hours of the night called Kaitlyn outside. Startled, she threw open the window and bailed through it before she was sure she'd woken up. The teacher crouched in the shadow of the schoolhouse roof. Her knees sank into the first layer of dust and her hands grasped at the ground to keep her balanced. She had the distinct feeling that someone knew she was there despite her black coat in the dark corner.

Past the school house, the full moon spotlighted the town. She strained her eyes, searching for what had been the source of the noise. A heavy Dragoon pistol hung inside her coat pocket, its weight pressing up against her side. She shivered, trying to throw off the eerie feeling of the night.

Though it was hard to see a black horse in the dark, Kaitlyn could hear Dolly shifting her weight underneath the overhang. The mare's reassuring presence calmed her owner. Kaitlyn's shoulders relaxed. Farther out, her eyes began to register a strange sight. A line of Herefords, five or six wide, walked down the street towards the railroad yard. Kaitlyn recognized the herd immediately. They were her family's animals.

The cattle passed quietly, almost silently. They had taken this road once before and knew where to go. Kaitlyn wondered why the boys hadn't waited until morning to load the cows. Perhaps Wylie had given in and increased his offer after all. Maybe Josh was in a rush to make the exchange before Wylie changed his mind. Then again, it might have been Josh who had caved.

Kaitlyn perched in the still night, watching the cattle go. It was a long show, and she sat observing for quite some time. Eventually, her mind wandered. It was strange to think about how her whole world revolved around animals. They had always taken care of her as long as she had taken care of them.

The cattle were the reason her family lived in Montana, and the horses were the reason she needed to go home. The ranch life might be simple, but it was in her. It wasn't just in her blood. It was more profound than that. Some spiritual part of her knew it was what she was called to do. She had been out into another part of the world now. She had seen what it had to offer. Ultimately, she wasn't interested. She was going home.

When the last heifer had been loaded, and the train whistle blew, Kaitlyn crawled back through her window. Once inside, the schoolteacher stretched out her toes. She stood barefoot in her corner of the schoolhouse, letting her feet feel the cold wooden floor. Sitting down on the creaky bed, she began penning a resignation letter.

The words came excruciatingly slowly. Though she taught others to write, the young teacher found she could barely muster up three sentences. After staring at the paper for ten minutes, Kaitlyn finally gave up any hope of writing a more eloquent resignation. She reread the three grand sentences and signed her name.

Kaitlyn set the letter aside and hid carefully behind the barrier wall while she took off her nightgown and put a proper dress on. Wrapping a blanket over her shoulders, she drank in the comforting hum of familiar voices that popped up in the next room. Confusion overcame her.

She could hear Josh and Garret murmuring around the corner but couldn't make out what they were saying. There was no way they could have gotten back from the train yard so quickly and without her noticing.

"Garret? Josh?" she called. "Are you decent?"

"Nope. Josh slept naked as a jaybird," Garret called back. She could hear Garret chuckling under his breath and Josh punching him in the arm.

"Knock it off," Josh snapped. "Yes, we're decent," he called. "Come on out."

Kaitlyn poked her head into the main schoolroom to see both cowboys propped up on their bedrolls. Garret's boots were off. Josh was still rubbing the sleep out of his eyes.

"If you're still here, who is loading the cows?" Kaitlyn asked.

Josh's expression was blank. He rubbed his eyes a little harder and looked at her again. "What?" he asked.

Kaitlyn reworded her question. "Did you have the other men load the cows?"

Both Garret and Josh looked at her like she'd lost her mind. "We're not selling them here, Kaitlyn," Garret said. "Remember, we're trailing them back up to Butte."

"I'm serious," Kaitlyn insisted. "I just saw all of the heifers get loaded on the train. I watched them!"

Garret sprang off of the floor, his eyes full of panic. He raced to his cowboy boots, slamming his feet into one then the other. His pant legs crumpled up around the tops of his boots, but he didn't bother to fix them. With a longer stride, Josh caught up and beat him out the door.

Kaitlyn was left standing in the schoolhouse, dumbfounded. She tried to shake off the confusion, but it clung to her. With no clue what was going on, Kaitlyn decided to follow Josh and Garret's mad dash.

She fumbled over their bedrolls and made her way outside. Looking down the street, she saw the two cowboys were still sprinting full force. They were almost to the stockyard already, and she wasn't going to be able to catch them before they got there. She watched them disappear into Wylie's offices.

"Kate? Is everything okay?" a voice called out. Kaitlyn looked around to see Lacey on her front porch looking concerned. "Well," Kaitlyn stuttered. "I'm not exactly sure."

Josh and Garret burst through the office door. Even at the early hour, Wylie was already at his desk. A plate of rolls and jelly took the place of his ashtray. He was halfway through a messy bite when Josh pulled a chair out roughly and sat down. Garret stood, arms crossed, blocking the doorway.

"Ah. You must be here for a receipt" Wylie said. He spoke with his mouth full, and he didn't seem to notice his intruders were breathing heavily. "Your man said he wouldn't need one," he shook his head and continued chewing, "but I knew somebody would be coming back for it."

The foreman glared silently, collecting his thoughts, trying to piece everything together. "Where are my cows?" he demanded.

"My cows," Wylie replied, "are on a train bound for Kansas." He reached into his desk.

With a smug expression, he presented a handwritten Bill of Sale.

Josh picked the paper up hastily. He half expected the phony bill of sale to disintegrate in his fingers, but it only stared at him. The words "Eighty dollars a head," and "sale effective immediately." jumped off of the page. At the bottom, the signature line read, "Agent: William Hofstede."

"We didn't have a deal," Josh growled through barred teeth.

Wylie shook his head. "This paper says otherwise. The cattle are already paid for."

"But he's not allowed to sell them!" Josh yelled. "They're not his cattle! He's not the trail boss. I am!" His voice had risen to a deafening level.

"I suggest you take that up with your crew," Wylie shouted back. "The cattle are already gone."

Josh leaped across the desk and was half an inch from having his hands around Wylie's neck when Garret pulled him back.

"Josh, Josh," Garret yelled. "This is no use. We're going to get the sheriff." the shorter but heavier ranch hand drug Josh through the door and closed it hurriedly. Garret placed a hand on either of Josh's shoulders and shook him firmly.

"Get. A. Grip," Garret enunciated the words deliberately. "We need to find Hofstede and the sheriff and get this straightened out. You putting a hole in Wylie's face isn't going to help our case. Now I'll track down Hofstede if you want to find the sheriff."

Realizing he was so tense he hadn't taken a breath in nearly a minute, Josh sighed. Composing himself, he trudged down the street in search of the jailhouse.

Dillon law enforcement left something to be desired. It took a considerable amount of effort just to find the jail. It was back off of the town's main street on a narrow dead-end of its own. Inside, the grand building was all but empty. It was neglected and sad, but it had apparently been an expensive work of architecture not all that long ago.

Josh wandered the hall, looking for any sign of a sheriff, a deputy, or even a prisoner. The only things he found were rows of paintings and sculptures that lined the halls, collecting dust.

"I think I know where the money for the school went," Josh said to himself dryly. He finally rounded a corner and found a room with someone in it.

The open door had a scratched nameplate that read, "Deputy Lee." An obese, balding man with an unpleasant expression was casually shuffling cards in the middle of the room. The card player had cleared a spot to rest his elbows amidst stacks of papers. He looked so disinterested in even his cards that Josh almost moved on to find someone else to ask for assistance. He looked at the nameplate again before speaking up.

"Excuse me, sir," Josh began hesitantly. "I have a matter I need to take up with the sheriff."

Deputy Lee didn't look up. "The sheriff's not in town. He's in Dell at the mining camp." He gave his explanation as if it should be common knowledge.

The room fell back into silence. Josh stared at the floor and then at Deputy Lee, who still hadn't made eye contact. The bulbous man had hardly acknowledged that Josh was there.

"This is a bit urgent," Josh finally said.

"What is?" Deputy Lee huffed. He seemed inconvenienced by Josh's presence.

"Well, the railroad owner bought our cattle for a lot less than they are worth and the bill of sale he has is bogus," he began to explain.

"I can't help," the deputy shrugged.

"Its cattle rustling," Josh snapped.

Deputy Lee finally looked up, but he seemed no more interested than he'd been before. With the lawman's attention, Josh continued.

"Mr. Wylie's got this seller's signature from one of our cowboys, but that feller never had the right to make the sale. The cows weren't his."

The deputy rose slowly, his fat rolling out over his britches. "I can go talk with Mr. Wylie," he conceded.

"Okay, let's do that," Josh agreed, trying to move him along.

"Not you," the deputy grumbled. "I'll come to find you. What's your name?"

"Joshua Challis. I work for the John Heide Ranch."

"Where are you staying at, Joshua Challis?"

"You can find me at the school."

Deputy Lee shot Josh a questioning look, but he left without a word.

Chapter Sixteen

The tense feeling of an impending fight thickened the air in all of Dillon. Kaitlyn had completely lost track of both Josh and Garret. Not sure where to look, she sat on Lacey's porch, sharing a quilt with one of Lacey's house cats. The two ladies watched the street, quietly speculating.

"I'm sure they'll get it all worked out," Lacey offered.

Kaitlyn shook her head. "Something's not right," she replied. "Josh doesn't get excited like that."

"What about tall, dark, and handsome?" Lacey asked. "I bet he's got some passion in him."

There wasn't much of a chance to answer. Kaitlyn spotted Garret approaching on Old Bay. He was leading Pepper. A wiry figure held on to the saddle horn, making a great effort just to stay aboard. As they came closer, Kaitlyn recognized the foreigner who had been part of the cattle drive. His head was sunken at an awkward angle, and a glaring red ring marked the skin around his neck.

Garret helped the injured man down and guided him to the porch. As soon as He'd propped Sol up against the wall, he turned to Kaitlyn.

"He's gone," Garret said. He took his hat off and pulled at his black hair. "Hofstede's gone, took off. The money's gone. The cows are gone on the train."

Suddenly the reality sunk in. The figures loading the cattle in the night couldn't have been Garret and Josh. It had been the new hires. Kaitlyn stood slowly, feeling like she needed to do something but not sure what would help.

"We have to get the sheriff," she said. "He'll catch the thieves and get the money back."

"That's not going to happen," Josh's voice came out of nowhere. He marched the stairs to join the others on the porch. "I just caught up with Dillon's excuse for a lawman. He isn't going after Hofstede. He said it's not his problem."

"There's something else," Sol spoke up quietly.

All eyes turned to Sol, all unbelieving that anything more could go wrong. The attention was enough to make him freeze up. The Prussian man was silent for a long moment, looking for the right words. He swallowed hard. "Hofstede and Lincoln took the horses," he said. "All the ones you left out in camp last night are gone."

Suddenly, a gut instinct clicked inside of Kaitlyn. She leaped up and rushed away without an explanation. The young blonde's cheeks flushed as she sprinted. In a daze, she rounded the corner of the schoolhouse to Dolly's pen.

The corral gate stood wide open. Dolly was gone. Kaitlyn's breath caught inside her throat. She sprinted inside the pen, though there was nowhere Dolly could have hidden. The schoolteacher turned circles frantically, looking for any sign of her black mare. Everywhere she looked revealed more emptiness.

Kaitlyn rushed back to the open gate and grabbed onto it for support. Dolly's halter, which always hung tied to the gate, was missing. Kaitlyn steadied herself deliberately. The logical side of her mind told her that Dolly had been stolen. Her emotions only registered that something important, something that should be present, was missing.

Feeling desperately alone, Kaitlyn dragged her feet, one step after another, into the schoolhouse. In quick succession, the young woman piled her few belongings into the old wooden trunk, drug it across the building, and left her resignation nailed to the schoolhouse door. She was determined not to look back.

Leaving felt surreal. Kaitlyn had hoped the moment she regained her freedom would be more monumental. She'd expected leaving to impress a strong memory. It didn't though. The feeling was no more noticeable than air unless focused on. Giving it all of her attention, she could still barely grasp it.

When Garret found Kaitlyn, she was taking turns lugging and dragging the massive trunk down the road a few steps at a time. He smiled at the comical sight.

"Let me help you there," he said. He dropped the two bedrolls he was carrying into Kaitlyn's arms and picked up the much heavier baggage. Kaitlyn felt the cowboy's gaze as he followed her around the corner.

There was a supply stage stop one cow path back from the main street. For an overpriced fee, parcels and persons could take the bumpy wagon ride between so-called "established" towns. It was a slow, uncomfortable mode of transportation but when it came down to it, it was better than walking.

Josh leaned against the waiting supply wagon. Sol was sprawled out on a stack of flour bags in the back. Burlap sacks wedged under his head acted as a pillow. Only the faint rise and fall of breath distinguished the man from the cargo. His eyes were closed, one from swelling and the other from exhaustion.

"He's going to have a bumpy ride," Garret commented.

Sol groaned in response.

Using the antique crate as a chair, Garret sat down. His hands held his sunken face, covering the bitterness in his expression. His sigh was a deep, mournful sound that could only come from a man who saw no other option – and didn't like the one he had. He finally looked up at Kaitlyn. His green eyes were empty and they shared an emotionless stare. Without a word, they knew the numbness that the other felt. Their state reminded Kaitlyn of going swimming in the early spring when it was still too cold to be in the water for more than a minute. Feeling chilled wouldn't cause any real harm. It was only when he didn't feel anything anymore that a swimmer was in danger of hypothermia.

Garret found a place on the wagon for their luggage then turned his attention to Josh. "We've only got two horses left between the four of us," he said. "I say you, and I go after some horse thieves."

The foreman shook his head. "Garret, someone needs to help the Boss with haying," he said. "We've already been gone too long. This was my mistake. I left the herd alone with those thieves. I should have known not to trust them. This was my fault, and I'm going to fix it."

The younger ranch hand didn't argue. The look on his face said he didn't like being sent home, but he knew Josh was right. Solomon was injured, Dorothy was still weak, and Kaitlyn was strong-willed, but when it came down to it, the equipment outweighed her. Without any money from the heifers, there would be no hiring more help. The Boss needed Garret's size and strength. The ranch couldn't operate for long without him.

Without much warning, Garret grabbed Kaitlyn around the waist and threw her up on Pepper's back. "Nice horse is a lot smoother than this old bumpy wagon," he said.

Pepper was significantly taller than Dolly and Kaitlyn felt like she was too far off the ground. She looked down, watching the cowboys say goodbye.

Garret shook Josh's hand firmly. "Godspeed, brother," he said. "Go get them."

The lanky cowboy mounted up fidgeted with his stirrups. The look on his face said that

292

he wanted more time to say goodbye but time was something he didn't have much of. Instead of speaking, he sent Old Bay into a steady trot. He posted with the rhythm of the big gelding's two-beat gait, moving out of the horse's way in hopes of keeping a faster pace.

"Good luck," Kaitlyn called out after him.

The wagon moved north. Its wheels rolled irregularly with all of the grace of a buffalo stampede. Garret sat on the driver's bench with his legs hanging over the side. Kaitlyn rode alongside, studying how his face had changed. More depth had come over his features as he'd aged. Though Kaitlyn had seen him only a few months ago, new sharpness was replacing the boyish cheeks. The cowboy's bare forehead was creased in thought, hinting the places that would someday wrinkle. Even his eyes seemed deeper-set but they were still the same ever-present green.

Suddenly, Garret seemed to notice she was looking at him. His eyes met with Kaitlyn's and effortlessly bore through her.

"It seems wrong to send Josh out on his own," the dark-haired cowboy mentioned. Kaitlyn looked softly back at him, understanding what he meant.

Kaitlyn glanced over her shoulder. If she focused, she could still make out Old Bay's tail trotting away on the far end of the bleak horizon. Before she could overthink it, she wheeled her horse around. Kaitlyn pushed her legs against Pepper's sides and felt a rush of adrenaline as the young filly burst into a rapid lope. They glided over the dry grass, racing to pick up the horse thief's trail.

Made in the USA
Middletown, DE
29 October 2023

41459789R00166